THE TENTH PLANET

Earth is dying as they predicted. It is dying of over-pollution and over-population. Only the adults can remember having seen blue skies. Crops fail, the rain seems to fall perpetually, entire nations starve, governments collapse.

A familiar theme? But it is not the theme of this exciting novel, only the curtain-raiser. The *Dag Hammarskjold* is the last space-ship to lift off from earth. It carries a precious cargo for the developing colony on Mars: scientific instruments, rare minerals, the seeds of specially adapted plants, frozen animal sperm and ova, and ten children of various nationalities and of genius-level intelligence. The last gift from the dying Earth to the young colony that is now mankind's only hope of survival.

The crew of the *Dag Hammarskjold* are Martian born, but the captain, Idris Hamilton, is an Earthman. Soon he may be the last Earthman.

The Tenth Planet

Edmund Cooper

CORONET BOOKS
Hodder and Stoughton

Copyright © 1973 Edmund Cooper

First published in 1973 by
Hodder and Stoughton Limited

Coronet edition 1976
Third impression 1979

Printed and bound in Great Britain for
Hodder and Stoughton Paperbacks, a
division of Hodder and Stoughton Ltd.,
Mill Road, Dunton Green, Sevenoaks, Kent
(Editorial Office: 47 Bedford Square,
London, WC1 3DP) by
Richard Clay (The Chaucer Press) Ltd.,
Bungay, Suffolk

ISBN 0 340 20512 0

This one is for Daryl Cooper,
my scientific adviser

I

IDRIS HAMILTON, MASTER of the *Dag Hammarskjold*, had been staring at Earth for the best part of an hour. It would have been better to have looked ahead, to have allowed his practised eye to pick out Mars and magnify it in his imagination until he could see the craters, and the mountains and the five cities, and the tiny, precious, man-made waterways. It would have been better just to have gazed mindlessly—as he had so often done—at all the pin-pricks of cold light in the black velvet of the firmament. But he had sentenced himself to look back at Earth.

He had looked at Earth as one might look upon the face of a dying friend. Correction—a dead friend. For Earth already wore its death-mask. No longer was it the brilliant jewel of the solar system, its iridescent oceans flecked with white and silver clouds, its continents glowing green with vegetation, its night-side cities bright with filaments of light. Earth was now wrapped in its winding sheet, its shroud of perpetual fog. Though, a hundred thousand miles away, on that grey sphere hanging in the void, there were many millions of the species *homo sapiens* who were taking an unconscionable time adying.

But, still, Earth was dead. When a man dies, the micro-organisms to which he plays host do not immediately react to his death. When a planet dies, a number of life-forms may yet linger awhile. Earth was dead; and the people back there, below that grey shroud, were, at last, aware of the fact. But they had yet to face their own individual deaths. They were not unthinking micro-organisms: they were human beings. They had the life-force and they had intelligence. Death would not treat them gently.

Idris Hamilton made the mistake of sending his imagination back down there among them. He shuddered and let out a great cry of anguish. Then, with a shaking finger, he pressed the stud that would screen the observation panels with duralumin shutters. He could take no more.

So now the *Dag Hammarskjold* was an enclosed world of its own, scurrying to Mars like a rat that deserts a sinking ship.

Hamilton sat on the edge of his contour chair, and tears coursed down his cheeks.

'I am not crying,' he told himself reasonably. 'I am master of this vessel and I am not empowered to weep . . . It is something to be master of the last space-ship to leave Earth. It is something to have witnessed the greatest crisis in the history of mankind. It is too big for tears.'

And yet, even by command, his eyes would not remain dry.

He broke the habit of fifteen years of space service. He walked carefully across the bond-fuzz carpet of the navigation deck to an emergency stores cabinet, one of which was in every compartment of the vessel, and took out a plastic bulb of whisky—or the alcohol, water and flavouring that passed these days for whisky—and broke the seal. Expertly, he filled his mouth with the burning fluid, not losing a drop. Then he swallowed.

Even as a wild young ensign, Hamilton had never sneaked a drink on duty. He had despised other men he had known who drank on watch. Now he had only himself to despise. He despised himself because he was a chosen survivor.

The whisky tasted bitter, made him cough. He drank some more. It didn't taste quite so bitter the second time. 'What the hell,' he told himself. 'The ship is in fall for a hundred and forty hours.' Which did not alter the fact that the captain of the *Dag Hammarskjold* was quietly going to pieces.

He remembered the time when you had to use magnetic shoes even inboard in a field of zero G. Clang, clang, every step you took. The noise alone drove some people round the twist. Bond-fuzz carpeting was better. It reminded him always of the time when he was a boy—how many centuries ago?—and used to throw hooked thistle-heads that stuck on people's clothes. That, of course, was on Earth—the dead planet.

"What the hell?" he demanded aloud. "I'm alone with it. Who's going to know? Who's going to know that Captain Hamilton, Distinguished Space Service Cross, seventy-five thousand space-hours logged, is falling apart? Brackley will be checking the frozen kids in the hold, Davison will be monitoring his precious atomic fuel, and Suzy Wu will be deciding on which culinary masterpiece to present us with for dinner, and which of us thereafter needs some old-fashioned therapy most."

"I'm going to know, skipper." The voice belonged to Orlando Brackley. "But don't let it worry you."

Orlando came floating along the navigation deck like a graceful bird. He hated the bond-fuzz carpets. He should have been a ballet-dancer.

"Sorry about that, lieutenant." Hamilton's voice was light.

"Captain, you think you're the only one with a wet face?" Orlando touched down gracefully on the bond-fuzz in front of Idris Hamilton. He did everything gracefully. Idris envied him. Youth! Youth! Orlando was only twenty-three.

"How are the children?"

"Cool. They do not complain. Life support systems function normally."

"And the lady teachers?"

Orlando laughed. "Ah, the lady teachers. Not just teachers. But the lady teachers. I like that. Well, captain, the lady teachers also are safely chilled and likewise do not complain. Let us hope that suspended animation does not affect their wombs unduly. Mars will require them to bear many children."

"Stop that!"

"Ay ay, sir."

"Forgive me, Orlando . . . It is an occasion, is it not?"

"Yes sir. We were lucky to get away from Woomera—evidently the last open space-port. It is an occasion."

Idris said: "Compound my felony. Help yourself to a bulb of whisky."

"Thank you, sir." Orlando took off gracefully and floated to the emergency cabinet. He took a bulb of whisky out of its clip and expertly gave himself a shot. "*Salud*, sir . . . How do we account for this illegal consumption of emergency booze?"

"*Prosit*, Orlando. *A votre santé. Grüss Gott* . . . You see, the dead languages of Earth haunt us even in our drinking . . . Don't worry about the tally sheet. There are two solutions. I will make good the loss from general stores or I will write in my log: this day, 23rd March 2077, two bulbs of emergency booze were used for emergency medical treatment . . . Yes, Woomera was a nasty business. You did not look out just before lift-off?"

Orlando wore a pained expression. "Captain, you know I didn't. I had to monitor the life-support systems of our passengers under the G thrust."

"You were lucky, Orlando. I did. The rebels brought in tanks and field guns. They blasted the control tower to rubble ninety seconds before we burned."

"Jesus Christ!"

"Another dead symbol. Jesus was a man of Earth. Long, long ago . . . We were lucky the pad was more than two miles from Control. They couldn't get our range in time. Otherwise, the *Dag* would have been blasted before it could lift."

"Commander Hillovan? Chief Worthing? That delicious computer queen with the fantastic boobs? What was her name? Sally Weingarten. What a hell of a name! Sally

10

Weingarten."

Idris drank more whisky, regarded the transparent bulb as a surgeon might regard his patient. "They are all gone, Orlando," he said thickly. "All gone under the hill, as some bloody poet once said. Hillovan, Worthing, Weingarten were blasted by their own people. They bought us enough time to lift off . . . Remember that when we touch down on Mars. Or perhaps I should say if."

Orlando raised an eyebrow. "Now I know who Suzy is going to cheer up first. We got away, sir. We are in fall. This is a good vessel. What the hell can happen now?"

Idris withered him with a look. "Anything. You've logged enough space hours to know that . . . But, specifically, I was thinking of sabotage. By my estimation there had to be at least seventy-five people concerned with loading, servicing and make-ready while the *Dag* sat on its arse at Woomera. None of those people had a snowball in hell's chance of dying in their beds, and they knew it. If, among seventy-five doomed people, you are going to count seventy-five saints, I shall call you a liar."

"Captain, the ship was double-checked."

"*They* double-checked—the security boys who very likely are now dead or dying. We didn't. We were too busy . . . So tell Leo Davison and Suzy they are entitled to a bulb of booze each, if that is their pleasure. But, afterwards, we all wash our faces and go over the *Dag* with a tooth comb. And, Orlando . . ."

"Sir?"

"You were born on Mars, I was born on Earth. If, at any time during the next few days my behaviour seems peculiar to you, you will assume command of this vessel and place me under restraint. I will immediately put this order in writing."

"Sir!" Lieutenant Brackley was shaken. "It is not necessary."

Idris Hamilton gave him a wintry smile. "Allow me to decide that. The night before lift-off, I checked internal security and then turned in and went to sleep. Next thing I

11

knew, I woke up standing on the pad, wearing my vest and pants, drenched in rain, surrounded by security guards. I almost got myself shot. They told me I'd been stooping and picking at things on the ground that weren't there." He gave a bitter laugh. "Matter of fact, I'd been dreaming I was a child at home, picking spring flowers . . . The lost flowers of Earth . . . So, lieutenant, it is an order and I will put it in writing. They must have taught you back at space-school that the effects of stress are often magnified in free fall. Therefore you carry the order on your person at all times. You will only show it to Engineer Officer Davison and Miss Wu if it becomes necessary to relieve me of my command. If, as I hope, we touch down on Mars without incident, you will return the order to me. Understand?"

"Sir! Yes, sir." Lieutenant Brackley saluted. He did not leave the navigation deck in his customary fashion. He walked smartly over the bond-fuzz, as if he had just been dismissed by a commodore.

2

MOST OF THE people of Earth never knew that their planet was dying. Most of the people of Earth—the teeming millions of Asia, Africa, South America—remained as they had always been: hungry, illiterate, disease-ridden, short-lived. By the late twenty-first century, man had established viable, independent colonies on the moon and on Mars. These were superb achievements of science and technology. If comparable resources had been applied to solving the problems that had accumulated in the terrestrial biosphere, Earth might have been saved.

But they were not. It was as if terrestrial man had a built-in death wish. As if the technologically advanced and highly civilised members of the human race, collectively, had shrugged and said: 'We're finished here. Let's toss a few seeds somewhere else, and see if they germinate.'

It was easier—politically easier—to carry out planetary engineering projects on Mars than to do so on Earth.

So the obsolete internal combustion engine continued to foul Earth's atmosphere; the pesticides, insecticides, herbicides and fungicides continued to destroy the balance of nature; industrial pollution continued to poison the rivers and the oceans; domestic effluent choked the antiquated, overloaded sewage systems of cities that contained ten times too many people; pestilence caught up with antibiotics; the demand for atomic energy grew at such a pace that waste heat pumped into the sea accelerated the greenhouse effect and brought about the melting of the ice-caps; and the vast majority of fifteen thousand million human beings continued to breed as if sheer weight of numbers would help them avert, rather than bring on, the final catastrophe.

The point of no return had been passed quite early in the twenty-first century. Many distinguished members of the international scientific community had given advance warning and had suggested drastic remedies—such as compulsory birth control, mass sterilization projects; internationally accepted limitations on the energy consumption of technologically advanced countries; the outlawing of the internal combustion engine; the reclamation of African, Indian, Asian and Australian desert country; the controlled harvesting of the seas; the re-distribution of material wealth and material resources; the abandonment of a costly space programme; the abandonment of the international weapons race.

Such suggestions might have worked or, at least, might have delayed the reckoning. But such suggestions were politically and internationally undesirable—so the politicians said. It seemed that they could only agree on how to tackle the problems of other worlds than Earth.

Thus, while Lunar City flourished and maintained a stable population of two thousand five hundred people by the most efficient hydroponics techniques, and while magnificent feats of planetary engineering were giving Mars a breathable atmosphere and the resources to support independently a population of more than ten thousand, which would be allowed to grow as the fertile areas expanded, Earth receded into a literally Dark Age from which it could never emerge while the teeming millions squandered huge amounts of energy on their hopeless struggle to maintain diminishing food supplies.

By 2050 AD the blue skies of Earth had become almost a legend. Nine tenths of the planetary surface were shrouded in mist, cloud, fog. Monsoon weather was no longer confined to southern Asia or, indeed, to a particular season. Overheated oceans produced constant evaporation which, in turn,

14

produced everlasting clouds and everlasting rain. Photosynthesis was an early casualty of the long wet twilight. Winter and summer became as one. Crops still germinated readily, but failed to ripen. The polluted rain beat them, dying, back into the saturated soil.

Since time immemorial, hunger had been a great destroyer of empires and the sophisticated ambitions of mankind. Now it became the universal destroyer. No amount of gold could buy a ripe field of wheat. Not even the most ingenious technology could create a stable window of clear sky for the dying fields and the millions of square miles of mud that had once been fertile country.

Eventually, even the politicians realized that Earth was doomed and that mankind's only hope lay elsewhere. Elsewhere consisted of two possibilities: a small, dead satellite that would require skills as yet undreamed of to transform it into a world where man might flourish, and a planet of immense potential that would take a longer time than was available to prepare for a mass exodus.

Therefore, with late logic, with late courage and with late resolution, the United Nations Organisation—ineffectual for more than one hundred years—determined to transfer all that could be saved to Mars. But the combined fleet of American, Russian, European and Chinese interplanetary vessels amounted to no more than fifteen. The largest, an American vessel built for orbital service, could carry one thousand tons of cargo; but that cargo had to be ferried up into Earth orbit in fifty-ton lots by shuttle rockets and then ferried down again from Mars orbit. Apart from the length of the voyage, the loading and unloading of the *Martin Luther King* took at least fifty terrestrial days. The smallest, a Chinese touch-down vessel, the *Confucius*, could carry a cargo of only one hundred and twenty tons.

The international arguments about priorities raged throughout four terrifying years, from the time when the United Nations officially authorised and supervised Operation Phoenix to the time when the last space ship, the *Dag Hammarskjold* lifted from Earth for the last time.

15

Should the Mona Lisa and a hundred other of the world's greatest paintings take precedence over semen and ova banks, the semen and ova having been donated by the world's most distinguished men and women? Should microfilm of terrestrial histories, of scientific records, of the cultural heritage of a hundred nations take precedence over sacks of plant seeds, specially developed for a low-pressure, low-oxygen environment? Should people take priority over computers, earth-moving equipment, high explosives, serums, electron microscopes, surgical instruments? What should be the ratio of women to men? What should be the maximum age for these candidates for survival?

Meanwhile, under the pressure of an impending Doomsday, old feuds flared anew. In a final and abortive attempt at genocide, the Pan-Arab Federation threatened to use atomic weapons on any space-port that permitted Israelis to lift off for Mars. The Chinese delegate to the United Nations demanded proportional racial representation in all emigration quotas—a natural demand, since the Chinese constituted one quarter of mankind; but quite impossible to meet when other criteria were considered. The Negro bloc also claimed that choice of survivors was being made on the basis of race prejudice, and threatened to blast any vessel out of space if fifteen per cent of its crew and passengers were not black. The Pope requested that two hundred dedicated priests be allowed to take the old religion to the new world. The Americans and the Russians managed to co-operate harmoniously—which was vital, as both countries recognized, since, between them, they controlled most of the interplanetary space fleet.

Somehow, in spite of all the squabbles, space-ship after space-ship lifted off, bound with precious cargoes from a dying world to a world that was, as yet, in its social and industrial infancy. In a frenzy of inspired adaptation, six orbital space stations were converted into temporary interplanetary vessels and sent careering off to Mars orbit.

But, as the incessant rains continued to beat down on Earth from dark grey skies, destroying crops, destroying

16

hope, law and order began to disintegrate. The United States of Europe was the first major casualty. Most of its over-populated countries had traditionally relied upon importing almost half their food requirements in exchange for manufactured goods. But, in the late twenty-first century, a fat chicken and a pound of wheat flour, became worth more than a Rolls Royce hovercar or even a Mercedes helibus. So Europe starved to death, noisily, violently. And after Europe, the United States fell; and then Russia, South America, and China. India, whose people had always had to contend with disease and starvation, lasted a little longer. But not much longer.

Oddly, the last country to fall into anarchy was Australia. By a quirk of fate, it had received most of the available sunlight. For a brief span, its deserts had become fertile and, seizing the opportunity, it had managed to grow enough crops to support nearly two thirds of its people. Then the skies closed, and the rains that had brought a brief period of fertility, began to drown the land.

When the *Dag Hammarskjold* lifted for Mars, Australia had just about reached the end of the road.

3

DINNER IN THE saloon was a very subdued affair, despite the obvious efforts of the crew to cheer up Captain Hamilton. Suzy Wu, genetically Eurasian but by birth a true Martian, had discarded her uniform—contrary to regulations—in favour of a scanty, translucent suit that revealed the contours of her beautiful young body to great advantage. She gave all her attention to Idris; but neither Orlando nor Leo Davison seemed to resent it.

Perhaps, thought Idris, Leo and Suzy had been briefed. It seemed likely that Orlando would have told them that the skipper was in a state.

He looked at the three of them and felt dreadfully old. He was not yet forty; but he felt ancient. These three were children of Mars. It could not matter to them in quite the same way that it mattered to him that Earth was finished.

Suzy employed her sex to cheer him up, Leo Davison employed his jokes. He told the one about the Englishman and the elephant. It didn't seem funny any more—Leo realized that even as he was telling it. There were no Englishmen left, and if any elephants still existed in India, they were rapidly running out of time. So Leo covered the disaster rapidly with a long, complicated, shaggy dog story about the Martian who went to the Red Hills to hunt the legendary abominable snowman. Idris had heard it before, many times, but he laughed. It was good to laugh at something.

Everyone, including Idris, was very tired. They had searched all the parts of the *Dag Hammarskjold* to which ground personnel at Woomera might have had access—which excluded the navigation deck and the reactor deck. Ever since saboteurs had rigged the reactor of the *Yuri Gagarin* to go critical as it lifted from Tolstoi space-port, it had been standard procedure on Earth touch-down for all masters to secure the navigation and reactor decks. Which, of course, did not eliminate the possibility of sabotage but at least reduced the areas where it could be carried out.

But, though the search had revealed nothing, Idris Hamilton was not satisfied. Something, he felt, was wrong. Perhaps he was just tired and therefore prey to neurotic imaginings. Perhaps he was in a state of morbid depression. Perhaps . . . Perhaps . . . But something was wrong. One important thing he had learned during his career was that a good space captain did not neglect intuition.

"Sir," said Orlando, "you have not been listening to a word." He sounded pained.

"I have." Idris smiled. "I assure you I have. The one about the Red Hills snowman was good, very good."

"That was two reels ago," said Suzy gently. "Poor Leo! You are just about the worst audience he has ever had."

"Leo, my apologies. You make a lousy engineer, and you will probably also be remembered as the worst bar-room raconteur on Mars—by everyone, except me."

General laughter. Then silence.

"You are right. I have not been listening. I was thinking about the search."

"Results negative, sir," said Leo Davison. "Not to worry."

"But I do worry. That is part of my job. The contract reads: the master of a space vessel shall worry himself stupid at all times . . . And, by the way, you are all forgetting the rules of the house. When we are not on duty, you call me Idris and try very hard to forget that I am an ancient Earthman."

"If you are off duty, Idris," said Suzy, pointedly emphasising his name, "you, too, must play by the rules of the house. You must relax and forget about being the big boy. Otherwise, the rest of us remain conscious of the gold braid on your dress uniform and the scrambled egg on your cap."

"Fair enough. I have stopped being the big boy, but I can't stop worrying. May we, my friends just talk a little shop? And then, after that, I will be quite happy to listen to music, make passes at Suzy or even endure some more of that dreadful Martian humour."

"Idris," said Orlando, "you are a neurotic bloody wreck. We understand why—not being entirely thick. You have two minutes in which to air your neurosis. After that, you play it our way. O.K.?"

"O.K. I'll make it short. The point is, the *Dag* is one hundred and twenty metres long and sixteen metres in diameter. Excluding the locked areas, we have searched it, the four of us. But can we be certain that we have been into every locker, every compartment? I want a double check. I want to search where someone else has looked and I want someone else to search where I have looked. There is something wrong, I feel it. If we find nothing inside the *Dag,* then we must look outside. It's dreadfully tedious, and I'm sorry. But them's my sentiments. End of message."

"You are thinking of the *Yuri Gagarin*," said Leo. "I understand things were worse at Tolstoi than they were at Woomera. Seems to me we had pretty good security down there."

"We did. But we are the last space-ship to lift off from Earth. I know that Mars will not be sending any more. I got it in code. Suppose the rebs —" No, that was not the best description. "Suppose my people, Earth people, Australians who have given us so much, broke that code? Somebody might feel very unhappy about it, being doomed to die . . . Hell, I'm talking about human nature." He looked at them all. "If you were destined to die in mud and everlasting rain wouldn't you be tempted to try to blast the ones that get away?"

Orlando shrugged. "I don't know. How can any of us

know? We have homes and families on Mars. And Mars has a great future."

"Yes," said Idris bitterly, "Mars has a great future — and Earth has a magnificent past . . . I am thinking as an Earthman. If I were left to starve and die, I might be sorely tempted . . . So, we will finish our meal and we will make jokes and we will take four hours rest. And then we will go over this bloody vessel inside and outside with a toothcomb."

"Idris," said Suzy sweetly, "you are a stupid bastard. I don't know why I like you. I must be sick. Somebody lay on some music. I'm going to teach this senile Earthman how to dance in zero G."

4

Idris Hamilton, space-suited, stood on the dark side of
the hull of the *Dag Hammarskjold* and gazed at a wilderness
of stars, bright, blinding, beautiful. A man could get dizzy,
space drunk, looking at such an infinity of stars. In the
early days of space travel hull inspectors had been known
to cut their lifelines and leap joyously into the void, eager
to embrace the dark secrets of creation. That was why lifelines were no longer made of nylon cord but of flexisteel. It
took time for a man to cut through flexisteel—time for him
to come to his senses, or time for someone to notice.

Idris was not alone. Leo Davison stood close by him.
They had both just emerged from the servicing air-lock and
were adjusting themselves to vistas no longer confined by
circular steel walls.

"Transceiver check," said Idris automatically.

"Transceiver check," responded Leo.

"Transceiver check," said Orlando from the navigation
deck of the *Dag*.

"Lifeline anchored."

"Lifeline anchored," repeated Leo.

Each man had clipped his lifeline to a recessed stanchion
by the service lock opening.

"Lifelines secured," acknowledged Orlando.

"There are only two places to which the groundlings had
access," said Leo. "They weren't equipped to give us a de-

scaling. So the only places they could have planted anything
—assuming anything was planted—would be —"

"The landing torus and legs," interposed Idris, "and the
area immediately round the cargo entry-port. We will check
together. The entry-port won't take long. Let's do it."

They paid out the flexisteel lines from the reels on their
belts and walked cautiously and awkwardly down the hull,
the muffled clang of their magnetic boots on the steel being
conducted to them through their suits. The cargo entry-port
was low down on the hull. Its internal air-lock had already
been checked. There remained only the task of examining
the door itself and an area round it as far as a man might
stretch if he were standing on the extended cargo platform.

Both Idris and Leo switched on their head lamps. Their
combined lights illuminated the entire area.

"Nothing here, Cap."

"No. I didn't think there would be. Too obvious . . .
Entry port search negative, Orlando."

"I hear you. How does Mars look from out there?"

Idris laughed. "Like a red marble—the kind we used to
call a blood alley when I was a boy."

"Blood alley! What a curious term! But it will never
be a blood alley in the literal sense, skipper. That I can
promise you."

"Promise again when your population outstrips the means
of production," said Idris sourly. "O.K. ensign, let's cut
the philosophy. We are now going down the legs to the
torus. We will each examine a leg on the way down and we
will take the other two legs on the way back."

"Acknowledged."

The landing torus of the *Dag Hammarskjold* was a vast
circle of titanium-clad plastic pipe. The heavily insulated
pipe was filled with helium. It looked like an immense
metal quoit, thirty metres in diameter. It was the shock
absorber that cushioned the impact of planetary touch-down,
and it was connected to the vessel by four great jointed
legs whose reaction to impact stress was computer controlled.

Searching the torus and its legs properly was going to

take a long time.

Actually, thought Idris as he walked slowly along one of the fat legs, it was possible to be too cautious. Since no inspection or repair work had been carried out at Woomera it did not seem likely that any of the ground crew could have gained access to the upper legs. They would have needed to use a mobile maintenance rig. But it would have been possible for an agile man, having the use of a rope, to haul himself to the top of the torus. Or if, for example, he had the use of a duralumin extension ladder, he might be able to plant something on the first three or four metres of one of the legs. Though there could be no valid reason for such an operation when a bomb on the torus itself would do all the damage that was needed.

Idris looked at Leo Davison, silhouetted against the stars, walking along his leg like some surrealistic insect of the night.

"Don't bother with any part of the leg north of the joint," he called. "I've not been thinking properly. A mobile rig would have been needed for anyone to plant something so high."

"Ay ay, sir."

"And, Leo—humour me. Give your section a real going over."

"Yes, captain." There was a note of resentment in his voice. Idris cursed himself for a fool. Of course Leo Davison would search diligently. He was a good spaceman.

They worked in silence for a while. The going was slow. On the sun side of the torus everything was blinding white and the phototropic visor of a space-suit helmet could not entirely take out the glare. On the dark side there was total blackness; and even with the headlamp switched on, it took time for the eyes to adjust. Idris realised that he and Leo Davison were going to be very tired men before they had completed the search. Afterwards, he resolved, he would make peace with his engineer. He would invite Davison to his cabin and, between them, they would broach a bottle of real whisky. Idris had two bottles of genuine Scotch left.

24

It was sacrilege to have to draw the amber fluid out of the bottle with plastic bulbs and then squirt it into your mouth like a bloody throat spray, but that was one of the penalties of space life.

While he contemplated the delicious prospect of real whisky, he methodically searched his section of the torus.

I am a neurotic fool, he thought after a time. There are no bombs; and I have clearly spent too much of my life in space. I'm too old for the game. When we touch down on Mars, I'll get myself a desk job.

"Captain!" Davison's voice cut urgently into his thoughts. "I've found something. It's clamped to the steel collar of Number Three leg just above the pressure distributor on the torus."

"What does it look like?" So! The hell with neuroses. Good, old-fashioned intuition had been right after all.

"Something like a small ingot—about twenty centimetres by ten by five . . . Some kind of limpet mine, I imagine."

"Don't do anything. Don't touch it. I'm on my way . . . You recording this, Orlando?"

"Yes, sir."

"Good. I will inspect the device. Have Suzy Wu place a laser torch in the air-lock. We may need it."

"Yes, sir. Be careful."

Idris laughed. "Joke! This will teach you all to think I'm slipping. I'll accept apologies in due course . . . Leo!"

"Sir."

"Don't touch the damn thing. Wait. I'll be with you in about thirty seconds."

Idris Hamilton was standing on the sun side of the torus by the base of Number One leg. He could just make out the black column of Number Three, and the figure crouching at its base, by the absence of stars. The walk along the torus would be a tricky operation. Titanium does not react to magnetism; but steel discs had been embedded in the titanium cladding so that some purchase could be obtained for magnetic space boots. The trouble was, if you hurried you were likely to take off into space then have to haul yourself back by the lifeline and start from square one, half-way up the hull.

Idris moved his feet cautiously, feeling for the pull of the steel discs, travelling as fast as he conveniently could. He swayed on his feet like a drunken man. Twice he almost lost contact with the torus. Eventually, he reached Number Three. His headlamp revealed a small metallic object shaped like an old-fashioned brick.

"What do you make of it, sir?" asked Leo Davison anxiously.

"Same as you. I'm not a specialist in explosive devices. But clearly it is some kind of limpet mine. No man would risk death to plant a heavily disguised box of chocolates here."

"What shall we do?"

Idris thought for a moment or two. "It may blow the torus, but it can't blow the *Dag*. If we lose the torus we can still go into Mars orbit and get ferried down . . . On the other hand, it may be possible to jettison this thing. Trouble is, we don't know if it operates on a timing mechanism, a disturbance stimulus, or both . . . I think we are going to have to play safe, Leo. We'll just have to torch that section of the leg off and send it on its merry way. We are already travelling at s.e.v. So, if we jettison, it is bound to go clean out of the system." He gave a bitter laugh. "Sad, isn't it? The only message we send out to the stars is a bloody un-exploded bomb."

"Sir, with respect, it is not relevant that the *Dag* is at solar escape velocity. The bomb can't hit Mars, and anywhere else doesn't matter. The only thing that matters is whether we can save the *Dag* intact. It would be a damned shame if we have to leave the ship in orbit just because some dead nut on Earth wanted his bit of revenge."

"What are your recommendations, Leo?"

"It has to be a magnetic clamp. Otherwise, why plant it on the steel collar? If it is a chemical bond, they could have fixed it to the titanium skin of the torus."

"So?"

"So I can prize it loose, captain. Then we chuck it away and forget about it."

"Too risky. For all we know, it could be programmed to detonate upon interference."

"It could also be programmed to blow any moment, sir. Torching it off the leg is going to take a couple of hours. We'd look damn silly if the thing goes pop while we are cutting through the steel."

"The possibility has to be accepted," admitted Idris. "But it contains less risk. So let us not waste valuable time. You will continue the search to see if we have any more of these charming souvenirs, while I collect the laser torch. When I have the torch and am in position, you will abandon the search if incomplete and get back inboard."

"Sir," expostulated Davison, "as Engineer Officer it is my duty to —"

"Laddie," said Idris, "I am about twice your age, I am master of this vessel, and I am backing my own hunch. Orlando is monitoring our conversation. You have your orders."

"Yes, sir."

"Well, then. On with the show." Idris turned awkwardly and began to retrace his steps on the torus. As he moved, his lifeline automatically reeled itself in.

He was back at the base of Number One leg and about to go back along it when Leo Davison came in once more.

"Idris—for the record—I'm about to disobey your orders. I have tried my jemmy under one end of the bomb. It lifted a little. If I can work the jemmy a little further underneath, I'll have the whole thing clear. When we are inboard, you can log me for mutiny but you will still owe me a bloody large whisky."

"Leo, don't —"

Idris glanced back across the torus. There was no point in completing his sentence. He saw a brilliant flash of light. The titanium cladding of the torus conducted the shock of the explosion to his boots; and the dull crump reverberated in his helmet.

He saw something grotesque spin out from the dark side of the vessel into sunlight. It was a nightmare. It was the remains of a man in a shattered space-suit.

Leo Davison had been eviscerated by the explosion. His entrails streamed out from his stomach like bright tattered ribbons, dripping globules of blood and fluid that froze almost instantly, glittering like crystals of red fire in the sunlight.

Arms akimbo, the body rotated slowly, drifting astern under the force of the blast.

Idris wanted to vomit; but to be sick in a space-suit was a certain sentence of death. He forced back the nausea, but compelled himself to watch. The rotating figure dwindled rapidly as it was propelled away into the blackness, until it seemed like a bright star, then a faint star, then no more than a pinpoint of light dissolving in a jet infinity.

Idris became aware that Orlando was calling him frantically.

"Captain! Captain Hamilton! Please answer! Do you hear me? Urgently request acknowledgement."

"Sorry, Orlando. My mind seized up. Leo is dead. He blew himself trying to get the bomb off Three leg." He peered into the blackness, turning his head lamp to maximum power. "Three leg is deformed and the torus is ruptured. There seems little point in making a complete investigation now. I'm coming inboard. I've had enough."

There were tears in his eyes; but they wouldn't roll down his cheeks because of zero gravity. They just filmed over his eyeballs, partially blinding him. That wouldn't do. He had to see clearly in order to get back into the *Dag*. He shook his head violently in the space suit. Some of the tiny globules splattered on his visor. Some just floated about until he inhaled them, coughing a little. Well, at least it was a new sensation, he told himself grimly—to choke on one's own tears.

5

THE NEWS OF the disaster had been beamed to Mars, the second internal search had been carried out with negative results, and a wake was held for Leo.

The wake was boozy and light-hearted—or, at least, superficially light-hearted—as Leo would have wanted it to be. They did not mourn his death so much as celebrate his life. Orlando recalled how he and Leo had gone on a splendid drinking jag at the nearest bar to Goddard Field while waiting to see if they would be selected for the shoot to Earth. Almost single-handed Leo had taken on and totally routed four white Martians who had loudly proclaimed that black Martians were inferior. Leo, who was black, had not started the fight. Orlando, being white, had politely asked the offending four to calm down. One of them had thrown beer in his face and another had kicked him in the stomach. At which point Leo went into action—Leo with his Master's Degree in Nuclear Engineering and his utter hatred of violence.

The way Orlando told it, Leo, the self-declared pacifist, became transformed instantly into a machine of destruction. He had used his hard negro skull like a hammer of vengeance, butting the face of the man who had kicked Orlando so that he fell back with a broken nose and blood streaming from a smashed mouth. While Orlando was still on the deck, another of the rough-house boys came at Leo with a broken bottle. He never arrived. A one-foot reverse drop-kick caught him in the throat. He gurgled briefly, then went down like a felled tree. By which time the remaining two were making for the door. By which time also, Orlando had recovered enough to grab one, while Leo locked the other in a terrible bear-hug.

"This inferior black Martian," he said softly, "resents the way you spilled beer over my white friend. It was a terrible waste of beer, to say nothing of the mild indignity suffered by my friend. Go to sleep, little man. Go to sleep." Then Leo's muscles had tightened. The man he held gave a despairing cry, a strangled cough. His face became red, then slowly turned blue. His head lolled, and Leo released the hold, letting him slide down unconscious.

Leo looked at Orlando, who still held his man but had not inflicted any damage.

"You going to put him to sleep, Orlando?"

"I don't think so, Leo. He's had a bad time watching what you did to his friends."

Leo had smiled. "Orlando, that is your pleasure. It is my pleasure to speak him a few words." He gazed into the terrified face of the survivor. "Boy, you have comment to make on the colour of my skin?"

"No, sir."

"You think black is beautiful?"

"Yes, sir."

Leo laughed. "Boy, you are the most god-awful shit. Kindly remove your sleeping friends. Only one, I fear, needs hospital treatment. Unfortunately, they will all survive."

Orlando had looked at Leo with awe. "I thought you were a pacifist."

Oddly Leo had begun to shake. He glanced at the three devastated men. "That is why I am a pacifist. Now, for Christ's sake, get me a large brandy."

When Orlando had finished telling the story, Idris laughed, knowing that Leo would have wanted him to laugh.

But Suzy did not laugh. She raised her glass. "Black was indeed beautiful, was it not?"

They responded to her toast.

"He was a damn-awful engineer and a lousy, insubordinate Martian lay-about," said Idris. "He was our brother. He tried to do for us and the *Dag* what he did for Orlando in the bar at Goddard Field . . . Rest you, Leo, in the deeps of space, where black is always beautiful."

"Our brother was a poet," said Suzy. "Did you know that?"

Neither of them did.

She held a piece of paper. "Listen to something he wrote on this last trip to Earth. He called it *Thieves in the Night:*

"We have such pride. We do not hide
    our arrogance. We, the new world-builders claim
    that any Martian man is worth
    ten of those who caused the death of Earth.
    But now, hanging between two worlds
    on a rope of darkness there is time to think,
    to reflect on pride, on life and other transient things,
    to know that we are only grave-robbers
    approaching the tomb of kings."

Idris raised his glass once more. "*Salud*, Leo. You were also a lousy poet. But we get the message . . . And having successfully robbed the tomb of kings, we must ensure that we get the loot safely down to Mars. We shall have to park in orbit, that is painfully clear. And, Orlando, we may have to bring those children and their teachers back to room temperature. I don't think there is much joy in trying to transfer their life-support systems to the ferry rockets. Too hazardous. Also, we had better look at the manifest and work out a system of transfer priorities. The people first; but after them we will have to schedule the electron microscopes, the ingot platinum, the telescope lenses, the antibiotic cultures and what have you."

"If we have to resuscitate," said Orlando, "and the very thought gives me nightmares, it will have to be delayed until the last moment. You know the *Dag's* recycling capacity. With that lot breathing, we could have an oxygen crisis in less than thirty hours."

31

"I know. But, somehow, we are going to have to cope with the problem. And I want another internal search."

"Why?" demanded Suzy. "We have done two already. You are getting neurotic, Idris."

He shrugged. "I can't tell you why. I don't know why. I just know something is wrong. Prove to me that there isn't, and I will be pathetically grateful. Meanwhile, we have about sixty hours before the first power manoeuvre. During that time there is a lot of talking to be done to Mars control, a lot of searching to be done and the resuscitation programme to be organised. Those kids are our most valuable cargo. They all have I.Q's of two hundred plus. Mars needs them. Leo died for them. Let's do every damn thing we can to ensure they touch down all in one piece."

"Captain, may I say something?" Orlando's voice was hard, determined. "None of us has had any sleep for nearly twenty-five hours; and during that time you have been exhausting yourself tramping about outside. You know as well as I do that pep pills don't pay off for ever. You are driving yourself into the deck. Sure, we can all take more pills and go on another twenty-five hours. But we'll be out on our feet, and you know it. And that's when we start to make mistakes. In this business, little errors have a habit of turning into big ones."

Idris gave a sigh and rubbed at his bloodshot eyes. "Orlando, you are bloody right. We'll take three hours sleep, then back to business. We are no good as walking zombies . . . The trouble is, I know something is wrong, but I don't know how I know. Just too damned tired to remember."

Suzy yawned. "Three hours. That's a real vacation."

They were the last words Idris Hamilton ever heard her say.

6

IDRIS WOKE UP sweating, shaking. He switched on his cabin light. The keys on the magnetic panel over his bunk were in the wrong order. There were ten keys altogether; but the only keys that had been replaced in the wrong position were the ones to the engine room and the navigation deck.

He cursed himself for a fool. He must have noticed the different sequence subconsciously many hours ago. That would account for his persistent conviction that something was wrong. But how could anyone have got at the keys? He had kept his cabin door locked, whenever he was not occupying it, all the time the *Dag* had been grounded at Woomera.

There had been the sleep-walking incident; and he had been too disturbed to notice how long he had been out of his cabin. Someone could have seized the opportunity—yes, someone could! But this was no time for a post-mortem.

He pressed the intercom button, held the speaker to his mouth and woke Orlando.

"Have a heart, skipper," complained Orlando. "I have only just got my head down. What's the problem?"

"No time for explanations. Emergency. Be on the navigation deck in ten seconds."

"Shall I wake Suzy?"

Idris thought for a moment. "No. She's not familiar with instrumentation. If she pulled the wrong lever, we'd be in trouble. Hurry!"

"Yes, sir."

On the navigation deck, Idris said: "Get the sleep out of your eyes. We are looking for something that shouldn't be here. You check panels, floor, lockers, furniture, manual scopes. I'll take the computer lay-out, control console, radio-communications. Let's move . . . No matter what it looks like, if it shouldn't be here, don't touch it."

They moved. Orlando looked all over the bond-fuzz first. It was clean. Then he rolled back the shutters and inspected the observation panel frames. Meanwhile, Idris began unclipping the inspection panels from the command computer.

"Why the panic, Idris? Neither of us are in good shape. Wouldn't it have waited till we'd had our rest?"

"Maybe, maybe not. The keys in my cabin were in the wrong order—the nav deck key and the engine-room key. I'm very particular about the order in which I hang them on the panel. Somebody used them."

"How could they?" Orlando was now methodically going over the chart table and its shallow drawers.

"I don't know, but I can guess. Maybe some bright boy seized his opportunity when I did my sleep-walking act." He replaced the computer inspection panels and turned his attention to the control console.

Orlando was now working on the contour-berths. "You think some groundling was clairvoyant and knew you were going to step out to pick up non-existent daisies?"

Idris went to work on the control console. "It doesn't have to be like that. He, she or they could have had a surprise present ready, just waiting for a chance to deliver . . . And it doesn't have to look like the thing Leo found on the torus. In fact, it probably won't look like that at all."

"Now you are being really helpful."

"Wait!" Idris, who had been looking under the control console, backed out and stood up. "I remember something else. God rot me for a fool. I remember something else. Have you checked the emergency supplies locker?"

"No."

"How many bulbs of booze should it contain?"

"Eight half-litres."

"You remember we drank one each?"

"Yes."

"Orlando, open the door very carefully. Count the bulbs."

Every compartment of a space vessel that could be made airtight in an emergency had, by regulation, to contain enough emergency food, water and medical supplies to sustain four people for two hundred hours. The regulation had been drawn up towards the end of the twentieth century when a vessel bound for Mars had been punctured amidships by a meteor. No one had been amidships at the time. Engine room personnel had been about their duties, and the navigation officers had all been on the nav deck. The automatic air-seals had functioned instantly upon impact. The air recycling systems in the engine room and on the navigation deck had continued to function. But before the stricken vessel could be reached, its crew had died of dehydration and starvation.

"Seven bulbs, sir."

"There should now be six."

"I know."

"Don't touch any of them, for Christ's sake."

Idris went to the emergency locker, stood by Orlando, and regarded the bulbs.

"They all look the same."

"Yes, sir."

Now that the thing had been discovered, Idris felt extraordinarily calm, almost relieved.

"The point is," he said, "it didn't matter what the bomb on the torus looked like. There was no reason for them to suppose we would need to inspect the legs. But anything planted inside had to blend with the scenery. When we have disposed of this device—whichever one it is— we shall then have to look for something that we would normally expect to find in the engine-room. But something extra . . . Now, which booze bulb contains the big kick, and what is its mechanism? Any suggestions, Orlando? Timing device, or disturbance device?"

Orlando gazed at the row of harmless-looking bulbs clipped in a plastic support rack. "Both, I imagine. As you say, there was no reason for them to think that we would give the torus a going-over, so that one must have combined both systems. Chances are the fake bulb is the same. There is no hope of discovering which it is, because they all look alike. It probably contains a liquid explosive—maybe even good old-fashioned nitro-glycerine."

"My thinking, also." Idris gave a grim laugh. "We were lucky. That would have been one hell of a drink to swallow . . . Now, let's move quickly, but carefully. We don't know which is the fatal bulb, so you are going to unscrew the support rack while I get into a space-suit. Then I will take the entire rack to the main air-lock and ease it out. O.K.?"

"Yes, sir." Orlando was already opening the tool locker. "The operation is going to take about fifteen minutes. Do you think —"

"I don't want to think. If you are religious start praying. Who knows—it may help." Idris took one of the space-suits that, like emergency supplies, were regulation equipment for all compartments of the vessel. He tested the life-support system, then took off his trousers and shirt and began to encase himself in the cumbersome suit. Finally he locked the helmet on. Then Orlando had to talk to him by radio.

"I have taken the bottom screws out and left the top screws very loose. You can remove them manually. I'll check the air-lock and flood the compartment. Should I alert Suzy?"

Through the visor of his space helmet, Idris could see Orlando's lips moving. But the words he uttered seemed very far away. Maybe the suit's battery was low.

"No. Let Suzy sleep through it. I think —"

Idris Hamilton did not complete his sentence. As he went towards the emergency supplies locker, there was an enormous blast that flung him back against the bulkhead, momentarily stunning him.

As he regained consciousness, he saw Orlando, face distorted, blood vessels bursting, tongue protruding, clutching

36

at his throat, sucked towards a long narrow fracture in the hull through which could be glimpsed the dreadful brilliance of stars.

Orlando was squeezed by internal pressure through the jagged gap. Diminishing air pressure was behind him, the vacuum of space was ahead of him. His body was reduced to mince-meat as he was thrust through the narrow gap into the void.

Idris was sucked after him. He hurtled across the navigation deck like a bullet and slammed against the fractured bulkhead. But his space suit held—for a time. Then it ruptured. Then he died. But by that time, most of the air had leaked out through the gap caused by the explosion.

His lacerated legs and the lower part of his body hung grotesquely in space, while his chest and still helmeted head remained inside the vessel. Then the third bomb—the one that he had known all along would be in the engine room—went off. It broke the *Dag Hammarskjold* in two. And as the hull distorted under the stress of the explosion, the jagged edges of the fissure in the steel plate of the navigation deck were pressed hard together again, neatly cutting the body of Idris Hamilton in half.

The legs went dancing crazily off into the void, following Orlando in an endless frozen pilgrimage to nowhere, among the stars.

By then, there was total vacuum on the navigation deck. But the top half of Idris Hamilton's body was perfectly sealed inside what remained of his space suit. His sightless eyes gazed incomprehensibly at the ice crystals that had formed inside his visor.

Suzy Wu, fortunately, never woke up. The first explosion, strangely, did not rouse her. The second destroyed the fresh-air and recycling pipes connected to her cabin. She died tranquilly in her sleep, dreaming of a wonderful spring day on Mars when she and Idris and Leo and Orlando had gone into the Red Hills to look for edelweiss and the abominable snowman.

The life-support systems for the twenty Earth children of

mixed nationalities and of genius-level I.Q., together with the life-support systems of the two teachers, were cut off instantly by the effects of the engine-room explosion. The vacuum of space sucked the air from their chamber. Ice formed slowly in their suspended animation caskets. They, who had been almost dead, soon became clinically dead. There was little change in their condition.

The engine-room section of the *Dag Hammarskjold*, given a retrograde impetus by the blast of the explosion, fell astern, to fall eventually into the sun. The forward section of the space-vessel, with its cargo of death, journeyed beyond Mars orbit, beyond to the very limits of the solar system.

7

THERE WERE DREAMS, nightmares. Sometimes there was excruciating pain. He wanted to cry out, to utter great shrieks of anguish. But how can you express torment, how can you tell the listeners or the watchers—if there are any—that your sufferings are beyond anything that a man may be expected to endure? How can you communicate if you have no mouth, no face, no body, no limbs? That, too, was part of the recurring nightmares.

Frequently, he ran away. Not with his legs, because he had no legs. But with his mind.

He ran into other dimensions; into long-lost pockets of time and space on the far side of existence. He ran down insubstantial tunnels of memory, seeking a world that had once been almost sane.

He remembered blue skies. Not many, but some. There had once been a clear blue sky for about three hours on his birthday, his seventh birthday. It had seemed like a gift from God—that is, if you believed in God. His mother and father didn't believe in God; but when he saw the blue sky, he had believed, if only for a short time. Sunlight had turned the world golden; colours had changed subtly, become somehow alive. And he could remember birds singing. How they sang in that brief respite from the fog and the humidity!

"Daddy, why can't we have more sunshine?"

39

"Because all the factories and all the engines in the world have poured too much dirt into the sky. Because there are too many people, and they use too much energy, and the air gets warmer, then carries more moisture."

"Why does it have to be like that?"

"Because mankind is too greedy, that's why. Greedy enough to poison the Earth."

"When I grow up, I'm going to be a scientist. Then I can learn how to unpoison the Earth."

His father's voice had been hard. "No, son. You will not be a scientist. The scientists have made the world as it is now."

"What shall I be, then?"

"A spaceman, if you can . . . Go out into space, where it is still clean."

"What is it like in space?"

"Dark and silent and beautiful. And you can see the stars always."

"Have I ever seen the stars? I can't remember."

"No, son, you have not. But, with luck, you may. I hope very much that you may."

He knew what the stars looked like, though. He had seen them in old picture books, in paintings, on film, in solidoscope. His father was right. It would be a good thing to go into space. It would be very clean. And the stars would be clean also.

The sunlight was soon gone, and the rains came back, and the earth steamed. As they went back into the house, Mummy took Daddy's hand and he kissed her.

"Do you remember that first time we walked beneath the stars?"

"As clearly as if it were last night." He kissed her again.

Inside the house was a birthday cake, and a present—a beautiful scale model of the American space-ship *Mayflower*, which had taken the first settlers to Mars. That night, he took it to bed with him and, in his mind, made fantastic voyage through a clean, sharp wilderness of stars . . .

Like a boomerang, he came back to the nightmare experience that seemed, at least, to be one kind of terrible reality. It had to be real because it hurt so much. There was pain in phantom limbs, pain in a phantom body. He desperately wanted to open his eyes to see something, someone. He desperately wanted to be able to scream. It would have been something.

He was alone in a black, eternal torment. I have sinned greatly, he told himself reasonably—after all, that could be the only possible explanation for his terrible condition. I have sinned greatly, and this is hell.

But he did not know the nature of his sin.

Nor was he sure that the hell he experienced was part of the perverted Christian mythology.

Nor was he entirely alone.

"If you can hear me," boomed the voice, "think that you can hear me. Think that you are saying: Yes I can hear you. Think it very hard." The words were not in any language he knew, but strangely in a language that he understood. The words hurt him, they hurt him dreadfully. He recoiled in horror. He ran away again.

He ran away to the moon, to the newly established Lunaport Two in the great crater Copernicus. He was a cadet, and he had just completed his first operational shoot. So now he was a true spaceman, inordinately proud of the tiny, silver star that had recently been sewn on the flap of his left breast pocket.

He was in the Lunaport astrodome, sipping his first moon beer. Men with twenty stars or more sewn on their pockets smiled at him. Some even raised their glasses. They knew how he was feeling. They could remember the feeling themselves—the first operational shoot, the first star. It was a once-off, like making love for the first time. You never forgot it. Or if you did forget, it was because you were getting very, very old.

He returned their glances humbly, nervously, with great awe, knowing that he had been accepted into the great fraternity.

A man with what seemed like a whole galaxy of silver

41

stars sewn to his breast pocket spoke to the barman. The barman smiled hugely and produced a small crystal goblet which he filled with clear fluid from an expensive-looking bottle. Then he came from behind the bar and said gravely: "Sir, Captain James Howard requests the pleasure of your company and wishes to propose a toast."

He stood up shakily, left his beer unfinished on the table, marched stiffly to the bar, saluted and remained at attention. His mind was reeling. Howard of the triple crown—Mercury, Venus, Mars! Howard, who had made an impossible rendezvous with the stricken *Leonardo da Vinci* when her plasma drive folded and a meteor took out the radio and she was falling towards the sun.

"Cadet, stand easy."

"Sir!"

"You have just made your first shoot, I see. What was the first thing you did when you touched down?"

He blushed. "Sewed on my star, sir."

Howard laughed. "Nothing changes, boy. That is what we all did. We put up the star before we passed through the air-lock—hoping that everyone outside would think we were on the second shoot and hadn't had time to put up the second star. That is the truth, isn't it?"

"Yes, sir."

"Well, cadet, how much dirt-leave have you got left?"

"About twenty hours, sir."

"More than enough to recover . . . This goblet—do you know what it is?"

"No, sir."

"It is the Gagarin cup, and you will find one like it in every space-port you visit . . . You know about Yuri Gagarin, of course?"

"Yes, sir. He was the first man in space. He was a twentieth century Russian cosmonaut, and he lifted off from —"

"Cadet, I know the story. Legend has it that, upon safe touch-down, Gagarin's first drink was from such a goblet. As the story goes, he drank chilled vodka. You have made your first shoot, and it is now your privilege to emulate him. You will repeat after me the words I repeated after the son of Neil Armstrong when I had made my first shoot. Then you will drain the goblet in one. Ready?"

"Yes, sir."

"In space there are no Russians, no Americans, or any nationalities recognised upon Earth."

"In space there are no Russians, no Americans, or any nationalities recognised upon Earth."

"In space there are only men, made brothers by danger, united by the desire to carry the seed of man far from the Earth which created it."

"In space there are only men, made brothers by danger, united by the desire to carry the seed of man far from the Earth which created it."

"In the name of Yuri Gagarin, I pledge myself to this idea."

"In the name of Yuri Gagarin, I pledge myself to this idea."

"Drink," said Captain Howard. "Welcome to the brotherhood."

He drank. The chilled vodka went down easily. He had never drunk vodka before. It seemed quite a gentle drink.

Captain Howard said: "Well done, cadet. Now you are one of us. I will give you a word of advice. Go to your table and quietly finish your beer. If any of our brethren should offer you another drink, decline with thanks. If any should insist, say that you have taken the Gagarin cup. They will understand."

He was puzzled. "It seemed a real gentle drink, sir. Not like whisky or brandy. I could drink it again."

"Laddie, I have no doubt you could, but you would regret it. You have just taken on board eight ounces of one hundred and twenty proof rocket fuel. In rather less than five minutes you will be ready to blast off. I hope you make a good orbit. Remember my name, and remember the pledge. Some day you will offer the Gagarin cup to a young cadet. Tell him that James Howard offered it to you . . . Dismissed."

He saluted smartly. "Sir! Thank you, sir." Then he walked back to his table, sat down, sipped his beer. He thought that he was very lucky to have been given the cup by Howard of the triple crown. He thought also that Captain Howard had been over-dramatic about the effect of that cool, smooth, almost tasteless drink.

He wondered why several spacemen seemed to be staring at him strangely, some with broad grins on their faces. Perhaps they thought he had taken too much liquor. Perhaps they were amused by the fact that he was the only spaceman present with a single silver star on his breast pocket.

Then the vodka hit.

Later he learned that he had offered to fight two ensigns, a commander and a full captain. No charges were preferred. It was a tradition that any cadet, having taken the Gagarin cup, was entitled to disciplinary immunity for ten hours thereafter.

He came back to the place that was no place, because it was unending nightmare, with memories of the unreal glow of Earthlight in the vast crater of Copernicus, of the ring of saw-toothed mountains that were two miles high, of the pale soft skin and the large dark eyes of the first moon girl he had ever seen.

Because there was nowhere else to go, he came back to the place where he could neither wake nor sleep, where darkness sometimes erupted into pain and noise and light, where he was alone, though alien voices sometimes whispered or shouted inside his brain alien words he strangely understood.

"Be patient," whispered a voice. "We know that you suffer. But soon you will see and learn, and know that all is well."

"BE PATIENT," screamed the voice, echoing through his brain as if through great canyons. "WE KNOW THAT YOU SUFFER. WE ARE TRYING TO HELP YOU."

"Be patient," it whispered once more. "We have had to make many experiments that hurt you. But now we know how to communicate. Soon you will see us and speak to us. But now we must make you unconscious while the circuits are established and tested. We are your friends. Do not despair."

If he had a mouth, he would have shouted, screamed, pleaded, coaxed. But he had nothing, only thought and pain and fear. Then, abruptly, even those were taken away. Everything was dissolved into nothingness.

Then, almost instantly, it seemed, he existed once more. He could see. He had no eyes—he had known that he had no eyes simply because he could never open or close them— yet he could see. Mistily, at first, as through steamed glass.

It was better than the insubstantial vision of memories. It was real.

It was real! He knew it was real. Knowing was the important thing.

He tried hard to focus (with what?), to concentrate. The mist cleared a little, but there were still patches floating about. When he concentrated very hard, the patches seemed to implode. Vision became more stable.

He could see a girl. She looked to be rippling or dancing. For one moment, disconcertingly, her head and the top half of her body just disappeared like one of the imploding puffs of mist. But he thought about her very hard, and got her back.

The vision stabilised. She was standing there, smiling. She had black hair, and she wore a kind of short tunic which looked golden. She was beautiful; but then anything—a rock, a flower, a skeleton—would have looked beautiful after a limbo of darkness.

She spoke, in the language he understood but did not know. "I think you can see me. I know you can see me. The monitors register your reaction. Please say something. You can speak, you know. But you must try hard."

He forgot that he had no mouth. Then he had a bright idea. He imagined a mouth—lips, a tongue, a throat, a larynx.

"Who are you?" He heard the voice—his voice? It sounded high, falsetto, terrible.

"A moment, please." She darted out of vision, then returned again. "Try once more. The simulation was not good. You would prefer a better voice. Try once more."

"Who are you?" This time the voice was so low it sounded like metal scraping on wood.

"Sorry." She disappeared from vision again. "Now, I think, we will get it right. Again, please. I know it is hard, but help me. We have done much work to give you a voice."

"Who are you?" It did not sound too bad. Not his own voice; but, at least, a voice of which he need not be ashamed.

"Ah, you are satisfied. That is good. I like the sound of your voice . . . I am called Zylonia. It is the name of a very small flower which can bloom in almost total darkness. Do you like my name?"

"It is strange, but pretty." He realised that he was speaking English, yet she was speaking the alien tongue.

She seemed to divine his thoughts, and tried English—disastrously. "Ay hef stoodeed yor lengwish, bet it is herd, hoord—no, hard. No onny spek it noo. Yo know mi lengwish. Can you spek en it?"

He found he could speak in it, easily. "How did I learn to speak it? I did not know that I had learned."

"You were programmed while you were sleeping—no, waiting is the better term. We had much success with your language areas . . . Do you remember who you are?"

Such an innocent question. Yet it seemed to pierce him like a knife. And, like a knife held firmly and twisted, it brought searing, excruciating pain.

Such an innocent question! He realised now that the answer was one among many dreadful things he had thrust away into some deep recess of the mind . . .

"I am Idris Hamilton," he screamed, "and I died on the *Dag Hammarskjold*. What have you done to me? *What have you done?*"

46

8

ONCE MORE HE went hurtling into the dark, running away from everything. Running away with his mind.

Back to the *Dag*. Chess with Orlando, about twenty hours before touch-down at Woomera.

Orlando was two pawns down and would lose a bishop in about three moves. Idris put the bulb of beer to his lips and pressed gently. He pulled a face. Lousy Martian beer. No body in it . . . Orlando's strategy was terrifyingly indecisive. No sense of pattern. The boy would never make a good chess player. He didn't have the killer instinct.

Orlando said: "Don't think I've lost, skipper. I'm merely giving you a false sense of security."

Idris laughed. "I like that false sense of security. I'm a sucker. Incidentally, it is my professional opinion that you are about ten moves from an excellent resigning position."

Orlando sighed. "Don't quote me, but I think you are right . . . Idris, how do you feel about it—about making this last shoot to Earth?"

Idris continued to suck beer calmly. "It won't be *my* last shoot," he said. "Earth dies harder than you bloody Martians think. I shall come back. Many of us will come back. There will be a time to start again. You'll see."

Orlando lifted his beer. "I'll drink to that. I'd like to believe it."

"Then do believe it, ensign," snapped Idris. "And go on

47

believing it until we start again or until every Earthman in the system is dead." He took the bishop and didn't give Orlando a chance to resign. He found a way to achieve an elegant checkmate in six moves.

And that is how it will be with Earth, he thought. The Martians and the Loonies will write us off; but, somehow, we will produce a rabbit from the hat.

Earth must not die—at least, not permanently.

But what if no hat? Then, alas, no rabbit.

It was something he refused to contemplate.

Orlando and the *Dag* dissolved.

There was a girl on Mars. Such a girl! Not just big breasts—beautiful breasts. Living symbols of richness and fertility. She was Earth-born, but shipped to Mars before she could talk. So she was a Martian. Idris met her at a space-port hop. And loved her instantly. Her name was Catherine Howard—a splendid English name.

"Are you married?" he asked her bluntly as they danced. He did not then know why he asked her. The knowledge came later.

"No, captain. Are you?"

"No . . . My name is Idris."

"That is Welsh, isn't it?"

"My mother was Welsh, my father was Scottish. I am Australian."

She smiled. "Soon, I'm afraid, you will be a Martian."

He shook his head. "No. Never." He laughed grimly. "Perhaps I am destined to be the last Earthman . . . No, not even that. Earth will survive."

She shivered. "I hope so. But things look bad, don't they?"

"Yes, things look bad . . . Are you thinking of getting married?"

"Yes."

"Anyone in particular?"

She laughed. "Some nice Martian boy, probably a planetary engineer, with a big future and a dune buggy and a hovercar and a three-roomed apartment."

"Let's sit this one out. I'll get you a drink . . . Why not a spaceman? They are the guys with the best health certificates and the best brains."

"You wouldn't be making me an offer, would you?"

"Given enough time, I might. But why not a spaceman?"

"The answer is simple. If I really loved him, I couldn't bear to be separated by such immensities of time and space, not knowing when or if . . ." She faltered. "Why don't you get me that drink you promised?"

"Sorry." He elbowed his way through the throng at the bar. Cadets, ensigns, engineer officers, a commander or two. Shamelessly he pulled rank.

He gave her a glass. "The bar is running dry. There was a choice of gin and tonic, gin and coke, gin and ice. I thought you looked like gin and tonic."

"You thought right . . . Why haven't *you* married, Idris? After all, you are quite —" She stopped, not knowing how to say it.

He grinned. "Ancient?"

"I didn't mean that."

"But you have been counting the grey hairs . . . Well, I'll try to give you an honest answer. I have been too damn busy getting where I am."

"And where are you?"

He looked at the gold braid on his sleeve and shrugged. "You are right, of course. Nowhere . . . I would like to be married, though. It would be something—something permanent. Something to hold on to. Especially if there were a child."

"A child." Catherine gave a faint smile. "Somehow, I cannot see you in the role of Daddy, Idris."

"To tell the truth, nor can I. But I don't believe in God, and I have to have something. I believe our only hope of immortality lies in our actions, in what we do to and for others, and in our children."

"A romantic atheist!" She sighed. "This conversation is getting too damned serious. . . A fine father you'd make . . . Hush, baby. Daddy is fifty million miles away; and if you

are very good, he'll come and see you some time next year—
I hope . . . No, Idris, spacemen should not marry, and they
certainly shouldn't have children."

"I could give it up if I had the right incentive."

"What is the right incentive?"

"You."

"Me?" She was surprised at the seriousness, the intensity
of this man she had known barely two hours.

"I love you." He was amazed that he had actually had
the nerve to say it.

"Isn't this all happening rather quickly?"

"Haven't you noticed? All the serious things, all the
important things, all the dangerous things happen quickly.
Spacemen are trained to react quickly. That is how they stay
alive."

"You wouldn't stay alive very long if you had to ground
yourself because some silly woman with a belly full of baby
couldn't bear to see you shoot towards the stars."

"Try me."

"No. I'm no gambler. I'm afraid to play for high stakes."
There were tears in her eyes. "Damn you! You're the first
man to see me cry."

"And you, Catherine, are the first woman to make me
say: I love you." He raised his glass. "I am sorry. Forget
everything I have said. Let there be peace between us . . .
I will even drink to that unknown Martian planetary
engineer who is destined to give you what you want."

"I'll go to bed with you," she sniffed, "if that is what you
would like."

He took her in his arms. "We'll dance. That is what we
came for, isn't it?"

"Yes, that is what we came for." Catherine dabbed at her
eyes, and smiled at him. "You'd better kiss me. Otherwise
people might think we were quarrelling."

He held her close, then found that he was holding nothing,
only darkness. Darkness, anguish, loneliness.

He kept on running. But wherever he ran, however fast
he ran, there was no place where he could stay. No island

50

on which, like a mariner of old, he could find refuge from the dark waters that threatened to engulf him.

"Father, I've passed the medical and the psychiatric. I have an interview with the Board of Space Commissioners."

"Well done, sport. To hell with this confounded rain. We'll go into Sydney, and I'll buy you a beer."

Darkness. Cold darkness.

"What is your name?"

"Suzy Wu, sir."

"How old are you?"

"Almost twenty-one, Captain Hamilton."

"How many space-hours have you logged?"

"The regulation two hundred."

"The shoot to Earth should be routine. But the conditions we find when—and if—we touch-down, well, they are imponderable. It could be a one-way trip. You are sure you want to sign on for the *Dag Hammarskjold?*"

"Yes, sir."

"Why?"

Earth to flourish on Mars."

"You are a romantic fool, Suzy."

She was dejected, anticipating dismissal. "Yes, sir."

"But the *Dag Hammarskjold* is crewed entirely by fools. Sign here."

Darkness again. So cold.

What the hell! If you can't run any more, then for Christ's sake stop trying.

I want to feel wind on my face, he screamed to himself. That I had a hand in bringing back a part of the dying I want to walk on grass. I want to watch some youngster take the Gagarin cup. I want to listen to music, make jokes, very vulnerable. "I want to do something," she said desperately. "Something worthwhile. I want to help salvage a fragment of Earth. I can't properly explain it. But it would be something to be proud of, something to remember."

She looked much younger than twenty-one. Very young, kiss a pretty girl. I want to *breathe*.

"CAPTAIN HAMILTON, PLEASE RESPOND! I

51

DON'T WANT TO HURT YOU!"

The voice was shattering, the pain dreadful. What the hell! If you can't run any more, then for Christ's sake stop trying.

He didn't have to open his eyes to see. He only had to want to see, or submit to the ordeal of seeing.

She was still there, the girl who called herself Zylonia. He found he could control his vision quite easily this time. No ripples. No cloud imploding.

"If I am not already mad," he said reasonably, "I am thinking of going mad. It seems a good idea. I don't know what else to do."

"Captain Hamilton, you are quite sane, but traumatized. We will not let you retreat into madness."

He managed to laugh. The pitch was wrong, but the noise sounded roughly like laughter. "You think you can stop me?"

"If we have to, yes. But we wish to minimize our interference with your mental processes."

"Baby, you are talking to a ghost. I don't believe in God, I don't believe in immortality, I don't believe in ghosts. But you are talking to one. So how can you stop a ghost from declaring himself insane?"

"You are not a ghost, Captain Hamilton."

"So? I died on the *Dag Hammarskjold*. Tell me it was a delusion. That will only prove you have whistled up a mad ghost. Q.E.D."

"You did die on the *Dag Hammarskjold*." There was a note of exasperation in her voice. "But, demonstrably, you are not dead now . . . You are making matters difficult, Captain Hamilton. It was decided that you should be phased back into reality slowly, so that you would have time to adjust."

Again he laughed, dreadfully. "It was decided . . . Screw that . . . As far as I am concerned, you are just part of a dead man's nightmares until you prove otherwise. I know —or *think* I know—that I haven't got my own body, my own eyes, my own voice. All I've got—all I *think* I've got—

52

are my own memories. Now if you—pretty delusion that you are—don't give me a very convincing shot of truth, I shall do my damnedest to blow myself into the big dark, where there are no dreams, no nightmares, no memories, no nothing. So talk fast, because I'm listening but for not much longer."

"Give me a few moments," she said. "Your responses are being monitored. I must consult my colleagues."

There was darkness and silence. It was as if the girl had suddenly disintegrated.

"I'm counting to twenty," he shouted, being now unable to hear the voice he used and not knowing if she heard it either. "If you are not back with some very convincing information by then, I'm going to blow. This I swear."

He began to count to himself. One, two, three, four, five . . .

She came back at seventeen.

There was light; and he saw her black hair, her pale face, her golden tunic.

"It has been decided that you shall have the relevant facts. We hope that you will be able to accept them. You died approximately five thousand three hundred and seventy Earth-years ago, in the manner you recall. Your vessel, the *Dag Hammarskjold,* was reduced to a derelict hulk by three major explosions which we can only assume were caused by people who wished to destroy it and its occupants. The wrecked vessel drifted beyond Mars orbit, even beyond the orbit of Pluto. It settled into an eccentric orbit more than six billion Earth miles from the sun. That is where we found it. By an extraordinary freak of fate, the top half of your body remained frozen and sealed perfectly in vacuum. Even more remarkable was the fact that brain damage was negligible. So you will understand that —"

"That I am nothing but a colony of cells in a life-support system." He was amazed at how calm his synthetic voice sounded. He was amazed that he was not hysterical, that he did not weep, that he did not utter a great scream of horror.

"Is that not what every living creature is?" she countered.

"Good for you. Score one . . . The story becomes interesting. I like it. Five thousand three hundred and seventy years . . . Hey, maybe that's a record! Tell me it's a record. Then we can break open a case of booze and celebrate. Sorry, I forgot. I have no mouth . . . Now, let's shoot for the big one. Where am I—woman whose lips I shall never touch, whose tits I shall never fondle—where have you and your unseen friends chosen to perform the resurrection-and-the-life trick?"

"You are on the tenth solar planet, Minerva. Captain Hamilton, do not be cynical. Many courageous and dedicated people have worked hard to restore you to consciousness and to give you the means of communication. Here is one of them."

Another person came into his area of vision. An old man with white hair.

"Greetings, Idris Hamilton. I am your psycho-surgeon and you have been my life's work. When you were brought to Minerva—no more than a handful of desiccated tissue— I was a young man. I dreamed the impossible dream. I dreamed of restoring you to full consciousness. I have spent my life to that end. It has been a long, hard task. There were many disappointments, many set-backs. It is strange, is it not, that a man should devote his life to bringing another man back from the dead? The ethical problems involved are insoluble. If I have done wrong, forgive me. I can only say that the project seemed worthwhile."

Idris was silent for a while. Silent and humble. He tried to comprehend the immensity of nearly fifty-four centuries. He could not. He tried to visualize a young man who would devote decades of his own life to the task of establishing contact with the five-thousand-years-old brain of a dead spaceman.

At length, he said: "Sir, I am grateful. I am also angry, humiliated, horrified. My existence now is nightmarish, grotesque. Surely, you can understand that?"

The old man nodded. "It will not always be so. I ask you to be patient, to give us a little more time. If you still

54

believe that we have been wrong, that we have violated your right to oblivion, the project can be terminated."

Idris laughed. "An interesting situation! The brain you have spent your life resurrecting is granted the right to suicide. But what if I am morally incapable of suicide? What if I simply continue to endure in anguish or madness. Have you the guts to murder me?"

The old man sighed. "We have considered all such problems, Idris Hamilton. They weigh heavily upon us. There are no clear-cut answers. I, personally, believe that the project is worthwhile. But I could be wrong . . . You have been greatly excited—over-extended—by the information we have given you. The monitors indicate abnormal neural activity, and we do not wish to take risks. Therefore, it is my decision that you will rest for a while."

Idris tried to say something, but the voice would not carry his words. Then vision faded. He tried desperately to think. But his thoughts seemed to be engulfed in jelly. He slipped rapidly into unconsciousness, almost welcoming it.

9

IT LOOKED LIKE the master's cabin on the *Dag*, and yet it was not. But it was a good simulation. There were the two chairs, the desk, the bunk, the communications panel, the pictures on the wall, and even what looked like bond-fuzz on the deck.

The old man sat in one of the chairs, the girl in the other.

"Greetings, Idris Hamilton," said the old man. "While you rested, we have made changes. We thought you would appreciate a familiar environment. Also we have made your eye mobile. It is a great technical achievement. By act of will, you can use your eye as you would use a living eye. Also, by act of will, you can take the camera to any position you wish. It will give you an illusion of movement. But I recommend caution until you have learned to completely control your new powers."

"Thank you. I like the changes." Idris ignored the fact that he was a brain in a nutrient tank and willed his head to turn. The eye responded somewhat jerkily, but it enabled him to look all round the cabin. He saw a length of cable that led to a shiny metal cabinet. There had been no such thing in his cabin.

"What is that?"

The old man smiled. "That is where you live. The other end of the cable is attached to your mobile eye."

"Is it possible for me to see my brain?"

56

"Certainly. I do not think it advisable. But it is possible. Do you really wish to see a mass of grey matter in which countless electrodes have been implanted? That, surely, would be the ultimate nakedness. Be guided by me. It would not be a beneficial experience."

"Perhaps you are right," said Idris tightly. "Dammit, I don't like my voice. Can you modify it?"

"Easily. Whenever you wish."

"I want something that sounds more like me—like I used to sound. But that will wait. First, more questions. What about Suzy Wu? Were you able to resurrect her?"

"Alas, no. The deterioration of tissue was too great. I do not know how much you understand of physics. But you, fortunately, were in a unique position. The normal evaporative processes were inhibited by the perfect seal of your space suit. You see, in vacuum even a solid will —"

"Skip that. What of the cargo? We had twenty children and two teachers in suspended animation."

Zylonia spoke. "Captain Hamilton, we managed to resuscitate eleven children and one teacher. Five of the children have suffered some brain damage; but the remaining six and the teacher—though they still do not function at optimum performance, perhaps—are in excellent condition. When their suspended animation systems failed they were already at near-zero, as you know. Their air-tight caskets helped to retard evaporation loss, just as in your case. You will meet them presently."

"Let it be soon," said Idris. "Let it be very soon. They are my only link with the world I have lost. Who knows—they may even manage to keep me sane." He looked at the old man. "You, sir. You who are my psycho-surgeon. You know all about me, but I know nothing of you—except that you have wasted much of your life trying vainly to reconstruct a human personality out of a lump of cerebral debris. Do I call you Doctor, or do you have a name?"

"Forgive me. I should have introduced myself earlier." He smiled. "You may call me Doctor, if you wish. But I also have a name. It is Manfrius de Skun."

"So, Doctor Manfrius de Skun. I have learned that I am on the planet Minerva, the tenth solar planet. In my day, its existence was only a theoretical possibility used to explain irregularities in the orbit of Neptune and the terrestrial approach of Halley's Comet." He laughed. "But I'll take your word for its existence—just as I take your word for mine . . . Now, what of Earth? What has happened in more than five millenia?"

Manfrius de Skun and Zylonia exchanged glances. The girl gave a faint shrug.

Dr. de Skun turned to gaze squarely at Idris Hamilton's eye. "So far as we know, Earth is totally devoid of human life."

"And the moon? Earth's satellite?"

"Dead also."

"What about Mars? We knew the moon colony might not be able to go it alone. But we placed all our hopes in Mars. It must be a very flourishing planet after five thousand years. Earth gave all it could to Mars. There is —was—a planetary engineering programme that would give it a breathable atmosphere, fertile soil, enough water . . ." He stopped, seeing the look on Manfrius de Skun's face. "What happened to Mars?"

"I am sorry, Captain Hamilton. To you the young colony on Mars is like yesterday. To me it is ancient history. Mars is dead. My ancestors were refugees from its internecine wars. They lifted off the planet shortly before the final atomic holocaust."

"*I don't believe it!*"

"I wish *I* did not believe it, but it is so."

"*I don't believe it!*" His electronic voice, giving vent to explosive emotion, filled the simulated cabin with thunder, causing its two occupants to put their hands over their ears, while their faces distorted with pain.

"Please, Captain Hamilton! You are hurting us!" pleaded Zylonia. "You must exercise control, otherwise we shall have to introduce an automatic cut-out into your sound system."

He did not seem to have heard; but his voice became

quieter.

"To think of the billions who perished so that man might make a new start on Mars, avoid the old idiocies . . . To think of Suzy and Leo and Orlando blown to glory . . . And all for nothing . . . I can't believe it. I can't . . . You have to be lying, both of you. It has to be some kind of conspiracy . . . They can't have died for nothing. The entire history of the human race can't have ended like that!"

"Idris Hamilton, look at me, please," said Dr. de Skun softly. "Bring your eye close and look at my face. Tell me what you see."

"I see white hair, wrinkles, the face of an old man. I see tears on your cheeks."

"Look for deceit and conspiracy. Tell me if you find any."

"I see tears, unhappiness. Why do you cry, Dr. de Skun?"

"May I not also weep for the human race, for the brave and gallant people, long dead, who tried to give it a second chance? The last refuge of mankind, Idris Hamilton, is the tenth solar planet, Minerva. Here we do not try to build empires, we have no dreams of conquest, we live in harmony. Harmony, you might say, is our fundamental law, our basic commandment. We are a stable colony of some ten thousand people."

"Ten thousand! All that is left of a race that once numbered ten thousand million!"

"Biologically, it is sufficient," said Manfrius de Skun. "If it is yet again our destiny to breed millions, we have sufficiently diverse genetic material."

"What is your destiny, Dr. de Skun? Here on Minerva, what do your ten thousand survivors propose to do?"

The old man gave a faint smile. "To survive, Idris Hamilton, to endure. That is our main purpose. Simply to endure until we know enough about ourselves, about the nature of man, to avoid making the tragic mistakes of previous civilisations. But now, also, we have the *Dag Hammarskjold* project—the survivors from the age of disintegration. I will be frank. You and the others we have managed to resusci-

59

tate are to us living fragments of history. You are from the Twilight Period. Perhaps, by studying you, we shall learn what went wrong in human development. Perhaps the information we gain will enable us to define our own development programme." He glanced at the girl. "Zylonia de Herrens is an officer in our Mental Health Department. She has volunteered to live with you, to orientate you in our ways, to give you companionship, to learn from you. I hope you will find her a pleasing companion. I believe you will."

"Live with me!" Idris laughed grimly. "How can she live with me? I am just a piece of debris in a tank."

"We made this facsimile of your cabin, Idris Hamilton, as a reality-anchor. Zylonia is also to be used as a reality-anchor. She will stay with you, talk to you, learn from you, sleep in the bunk you used to occupy. As a woman, she will do her best to please you. As a scientist, she will do her best to understand you. Later, when you understand our society better, there may be a less passive role for you to play. That is all I can say now. For the time being, I will leave you, Idris Hamilton. Be assured that we are doing our best for you."

Zylonia said: "Idris, I want to please you very much. Believe that I think of you not as a brain in nutrient solution, but as a man. I have my own dreams, just as you have yours."

Idris Hamilton uttered a great electronic sigh. "Then we must each take consolation from our dreams. Thank you for volunteering to keep me company. It is almost an act of love."

Zylonia tossed back her hair. "It *is* an act of love," she said.

IO

THERE WERE TWO clocks in the cabin. One was the actual clock taken from the bulkhead of the master's cabin on the *Dag,* miraculously persuaded to work once more after an interval of five thousand years. The other was Zylonia's—a much evolved replica of a Swiss cuckoo-clock. She had had it since she was a child. Evidently it was a kind of talisman.

They were both twenty-four hour clocks; but they did not often tell the same time. The Martian day being longer than the terrestrial day, each Martian minute was almost one and a half seconds longer than each Earth minute. Idris amused himself briefly by calculating that once every forty-three days—Earth days—the clocks ought to tell the same time.

The standard Martian day, he learned, was still used to regulate the passage of time on Minerva, though the planetary period of rotation was almost exactly twenty terrestrial hours. It was used for sentimental, traditional and practical reasons. It was used because the first colonists brought Mars time with them, and lived by it. It was used because a twenty-four hour day—even allowing for the slight Martian variation—corresponded to the ancient cycle of human metabolism. It was used because night and day on Minerva were almost meaningless abstractions.

The planet, nearly six billion miles from the sun, existed in perpetual night. It was a frozen world. The sun, the brightest star in its sky, was too far away to afford any life-giving warmth, any appreciable increase of light. The surface of Minerva was permanently frozen in permanent darkness. The first colonists had burrowed beneath its surface to establish underground refuges, which later expanded into small cities. They had returned to the surface as little as possible, though they maintained a few scientific and technological installations amid the wastes of rock and frozen gasses, and even a small space-port.

The space-port serviced and maintained five small ferry rockets, used chiefly for short planetary shoots and for exploratory shoots to Minerva's only satellite, an irregular lump of cosmic debris no more than five hundred kilometres in diameter which orbited the planet at a mean distance of seventy-three thousand kilometres. There was also one ancient deep-space vessel, carefully maintained but rarely used. It was three thousand Earth-years old and had been part of the original exodus fleet from Mars. It had been repaired and refurbished so often during its long existence that hardly any of the original components remained. The last time it had been used was when radio and visual telescopes had tracked the wreck of the *Dag Hammarskjold*. Then the *Amazonia* had lifted off from Talbot Field to effect the most dramatic space rescue in the whole of human history.

According to legend and the known facts of Minervan history, the bulk of the fleet that had brought the Martian refugees to Minerva had been destroyed on the orders of Garfield Talbot, its commander. The exodus fleet, hastily assembled, badly equipped, was originally destined to shoot for the nearer stars—Alpha Centauri, Sirius, Altair, Procyon. But, to Garfield Talbot, an intensely religious man, the discovery of the tenth planet had seemed like a sign. The fact that it could be made to support human life, even if only subterraneously, seemed like an invitation. He argued that it was better for the refugees from devastated Mars to accept an austere but certain future on Minerva than to try to cross the light-years in the hope of discovering systems that might not exist.

So the original plans were cancelled after the fleet had been in space for less than two thousand hours. The fleet would not disperse to its assigned stars—which there was little hope of reaching anyway—but would touch down on the outermost solar planet, which at least offered a sanctuary that should not be beyond the ingenuity of man to improve.

One adventurous and rebellious captain refused to accept the change of plan. Garfield Talbot considered his refusal to be an affront to divine guidance, and promptly blasted his vessel out of space with an atomic torpedo. The remaining space-ships—twelve in all—obediently changed course for Minerva.

After touch-down, after the colonists had established underground bases large enough to support them, Talbot ordered the destruction of the fleet, his argument being that God, in his infinite mercy, had offered mankind a third chance. If the race of man could not learn to live in peace in the solar system, it would not manage to do so elsewhere. Conditions on—or under—the surface of Minerva were extremely hard. But that was simply God's punishment and his way of testing.

Garfield Talbot was forty-three years old when he brought the remnants of Martian civilisation to Minerva. He lived to the ripe age of one hundred and twenty-one, working with almost fanatical dedication for nearly eighty years to establish a harmonious and stable community. For him, stability and harmony meant strict discipline, strict adherence to the law, swift and stern justice.

He had set down his ideas on the purpose and nature of society and of human destiny in a book called simply *Talbot's Creed*. Over the centuries it had attained the stature of a testament. It was the only authoritative bible on Minerva. The Judeo-Christian mythologies had lost their significance even before the Martian culture had disintegrated. But the mythological parallel was obvious. Garfield Talbot, the Moses of deep space, had brought his chosen people to the promised land of Minerva. It was an inhospitable wilderness frozen in everlasting night. Therefore it was the perfect place for mankind to atone for previous sins and to establish a new harmonic order of society.

Since Garfield Talbot's great passion was for order and balance, Minervan culture had not evolved greatly in the thirty Earth-centuries that the tenth planet had been colonised. Government, in the form of the Five Cities Council, had found it convenient and necessary to adhere strictly to the teachings of *Talbot's Creed*.

Although a fanatic and a dreamer, Talbot had been acutely aware of the limits of the technological skills brought by the original colonists. Therefore he had ordained that the maximum population should be ten thousand. That maximum had been religiously kept despite new scientific discoveries and new technological development. Minerva was now capable of supporting one hundred thousand people. But *Talbot's Creed* was stronger than scientific and technological progress. *Talbot's Creed* was the law.

As time passed Idris learned much about Talbot and his influence on Minervan society. Also, he learned much about Zylonia, as a woman and as a Minervan.

But, most of all, he learned about himself.

II

"When can I meet the other survivors from the *Dag?*" It was a question he had asked many times, with increasing impatience.

"Soon. Quite soon, now." Zylonia gave him the standard reply.

He began to suspect a conspiracy. He began to think that, for some reason, the Minervans had decided not to let him see the surviving children and their teacher.

The trouble was he had to take everything they said and did on trust. He could not investigate personally. He was just a brain in a tank of nutrient. A biological curio wired electronically for sound and vision, capable of receiving only the data deliberately fed into it. He was a prisoner.

Perhaps the survivors did not exist. Perhaps Manfrius de Skun did not exist. Perhaps Zylonia did not exist. Perhaps Orlando and Leo and Suzy were still alive, and the *Dag Hammarskjold* was shooting uneventfully to Mars, and the captain was confined to his cabin because he had quietly gone nuts.

So, therefore, his deranged mind must have invented Minerva, the girl Zylonia, and the old man who claimed to be his psycho-surgeon. It figured. Paranoia was a distinct possibility for a man who had logged too many space-hours and who had had to lift a salvage cargo from his home planet before it died.

It figured. Yes, paranoia was a good solution. The *Dag Hammarskjold* had never been sabotaged. All was well. Except that Captain Idris Hamilton was busy creating three-dimensional paper dolls.

"How bloody long is soon?" he screamed.

Zylonia cowered, putting her hands over her ears. "If you are going to use your voice as a weapon, I shall have to turn down the volume. You will find it exhausting, Idris. You will always have to shout to be heard."

He was contrite. "I'm sorry. Even if you are a paper doll, I have to accept some responsibility for your existence. I'm sorry."

"What are you talking about?"

"I don't know . . . Or I'm afraid to know . . . Let's get back to the children and the surviving teacher."

"Idris, you must be patient. Please try to believe that our most highly skilled doctors are doing all they believe to be best for you and the others." She smiled. "Medicine and psycho-surgery have made great advances since your time. Otherwise you would not be alive now. But, if we are not to end up with mentally deranged people, the process of integration and orientation must be carried out slowly. Are you prepared to risk their sanity, as well as yours, because you are impatient?"

He was silent for a while. Then he said bitterly: "I have a choice of believing you or disbelieving you. I will try to believe you if only because it is less agonizing . . . But take good care of those Earth children—if they exist, and if you exist. I want to think that it didn't all happen for nothing."

"We are taking good care of them," she said softly. "I promise you."

"Well, then, Miss Zylonia de Herrens, take off your clothes."

"Take off my clothes?" She was amazed.

He enjoyed her amazement. He could feel himself enjoying it. The sensation was good.

"I want to find out what the sight of a naked woman does to me." He laughed. "As a scientist you should be very interested in the response of a brain in a tank to sexual stimulus . . . Or are you too inhibited? Perhaps Minervan society has a stricter sexual code than I imagined."

"I am not too inhibited," she said tartly, "and Minervan society is not riddled with primitive sexual tabu. I am reluctant only because there is your incidence of frustration to consider."

He was vastly amused at the thought. "My incidence of frustration! That's a pleasing phrase. I like it . . . Maybe if you Minervans had given some thought to my incidence of frustration, you would have left my corpse—or the half of it you found—to drift through the galaxy in peace. Strip, Zylonia! Give a few billion resuscitated grey cells a treat."

"I — I —" She was confused, and he enjoyed her confusion.

"Ho, ho! This is one of my good times. Maybe life is worth living—using the word somewhat loosely—after all . . . I presume we are monitored. It would account for your confusion."

"Yes — No. Idris, I don't think this is a good idea."

"So, we are monitored. I thought as much. But it doesn't matter. Let's give the boys at the video screens a bit of fun. Strip, child. No doubt Manfrius de Skun will have much joy deciphering the variations in my brain rhythms. Strip!"

He thought she would chicken, but she didn't.

Zylonia took off her tunic, her chemise, her bra, her panties. He was delighted to discover that such garments had changed very little in five thousand years. It was a great consolation.

Having committed herself, Zylonia at least carried out the task bravely. She placed her hands on her hips and stood facing his 'eye' calmly. "Does this improve your state of mind, Idris? Do you like what you see?"

He did not answer for a while. At last, he said: "I like what I see. It's a real tonic. It feels as if I had forgotten about the human body—not the facts, but, somehow, the idea. I am glad to be reminded . . . The body is a very beautiful thing. Seeing you like this is a renewal of intimacy, a kind of contact. It makes me feel less lonely. Walk about, Zylonia. I want to see the muscles move."

She walked about the cabin, a little self-consciously. She stooped to pick up the clothes she had taken off, smoothed them out and placed them carefully on the bunk.

Idris experienced real pleasure. He willed his 'eye' to follow her closely, lovingly, almost caressingly. The sensation of pleasure was intoxicating. It was the first time he had experienced it, since his resurrection.

"May I put my clothes on now?" said Zylonia. "Surely you have seen enough?"

"No to both," he said emphatically. "I have news for you and for those bright lads at the monitor screens. I'm enjoying it. I'm enjoying it immensely. Dr. de Skun will doubtless be interested to learn that, deprived of a body, a glandular system, any means of touch or fulfilment, this thing in a tank can still experience sexual arousal, immense pleasure." He laughed. "You Minervans are to be congratulated. You have created the most dedicated voyeur in the solar system . . . I'll tell you something else, Zylonia. I want a lavatory, a head, a john or whatever you call it, installed in this stage set. I see you eat and relax and sleep. I want to see you do the everyday things that people do with their bodies. . . . Don't you understand? You are my proxy. It is only through you that I can cherish the illusion of being alive."

Unaccountably, she began to cry. "You *are* alive. Oh, Idris, it won't be long before you can be fully alive. They are growing a new body for you."

"*What did you say?*"

"They are growing a new body for you . . . You weren't supposed to learn about it so early in the programme. But it's true."

12

HE SHOT HIS mobile eye very close to her face so that, for
an instant, she was afraid he was literally hurling the camera
at her by will-power. Instinctively, she held up her hands to
protect herself.

"Sorry! It never occurred to me that I could use my eye
as a weapon. An interesting thought . . ."

She lowered her hands. He looked closely, searchingly,
at her face.

"Now, make it slow and clear, Zylonia, because I am only
a stupid spaceman—or, at least, I used to be. How the hell
can they grow me a new body?"

"Do you understand anything of genetics?"

"No. But I am willing to learn."

"You have heard of cloning?"

"I seem to recall that it's a technique of duplication. It
was used on Earth, and on Mars, I think, for producing exact
copies of prize cattle. Beyond that I know nothing."

"The principle is simple," said Zylonia, "but the techniques involved are fantastically complicated. You see, the
cells of the body each contain all the genetic coding, or
design for an entirely new body. I know very little of the
actual process of cellular surgery, and we have only recently
succeeded in cloning from human cells; but given the right
kind of environment—in this case a synthetic uterus—it is
possible to electronically trigger the reproduction code in the

69

cell nucleus so that the development cycle begins. Eventually, it yields a mature physical copy of the being from which the genetic material was taken."

"So. You are busy growing a new Idris Hamilton. That's very resourceful. I can see I am going to be eternally grateful to all you helpful Minervans." He managed to get heavy sarcasm into his voice—and that, too, was a tribute to Minervan technology.

"Not a new Idris Hamilton. The seat of identity is the brain. You are Idris Hamilton. You only. No one else can be."

"Ah yes, the brain. A poor thing, but mine own . . . But it occurs to me that the zombie you are creating—which is, so to speak, my blood brother—will also have problems. He, too, has a brain—a hot little seat of identity."

"May I put my clothes on?" she said.

"No, damn you! I, too, exist in a kind of nakedness. But the sight of your breasts and belly reminds me that I was once a man. If you are going to live with me as my reality-anchor, I think you call it, then you can *be* real for some of the time . . . Now back to Idris Hamilton, Mark Two. What about *his* brain? Are you proposing to give me his body and stick him in my tank? If so, I don't think he is going to like it."

"Fortunately, we do not have such a difficult ethical problem. Your clone brother has never been allowed to attain full consciousness. We have been able to accelerate the development processes of his body while retarding the process of individuation in the brain. It is a magnificent achievement."

"A magnificent achievement? One man who was dead has been given a facsimile of living, and a man who is alive is being confined to a pseudo-death. All this, I presume, is to further scientific progress. If I had a mouth I would vomit!"

The door opened and Manfrius de Skun entered the cabin. "Put on your clothes, Zylonia," he said peremptorily. "The monitors are registering unacceptable response turbulence.

You were not empowered to inform Idris Hamilton of the cloned body. We need time to consider the possible consequences."

"Ah, the good doctor!" Idris brought his eye close to Manfrius de Skun. "I was expecting you. You are disturbed by the reaction of your guinea pig. So you should be. I have been thinking. I have plenty of time to think, you know. I asked myself why should a colony of ten thousand people devote so much of its available resources to resurrecting a dead Earthman? An interesting question. I think I have the answer."

Manfrius de Skun smiled. "Captain Hamilton, we realised you were a man of great courage and considerable intelligence. Such qualities are necessary for anyone in command of a space-ship. Also, you were expendable—or, more correctly, I should say expended—material. Therefore —"

"Therefore," cut in Idris, "I was an ideal candidate for your immortality project. Nothing to lose, and everything to gain. Correct?"

"Correct."

"For some reason," went on Idris, "you were denied the use of a Minervan brain—dead or alive."

Manfrius de Skun shrugged. "At the time—many years ago, you understand—there were political and philosophical objections. Ethical objections, also. Though we could infer electronically from the pattern of monitored rhythms how a brain was reacting in total isolation, we could not have subjective verification, at least for some time. It could be argued—and was argued—that an isolated brain might be suffering terrible torments of which we could have no knowledge. There were social considerations, too. Our community, as you are aware, is very small by the standards of your era. Everyone has many relations who are naturally concerned about their welfare. The experimental use of a Minervan brain would have brought too many complications. But, thanks to the progress you have made, immortality is within our grasp."

"So now you know that a brain can survive the terrors of

isolation without entirely losing its sanity. Bully for you. And now all decent law-abiding Minervans can look forward to the prospect of immortality. Bully for them. I, on the other hand, am not feeling unreservedly happy about my own condition . . . Also, I want to see my children, and their teacher."

Manfrius de Skun raised an eyebrow. "*Your* children, Captain Hamilton?"

"Yes, *my* children. I am of Earth, they are of Earth. They were in my charge. They are my children. You may have restored them to life; but that does not give you any right to determine their future."

"You believe that you have a stronger claim?"

"I believe that, since I am of their culture, born on the planet they were born on, I have not a claim but a duty. So let us stop swapping abstract nouns. I want to see the children. Don't think that because I am just a brain in a tank that I have no bargaining position. I can wreck your immortality project any time I want."

"And how do you propose to do that?"

Idris laughed. "Simple. By demonstrating that I am insane."

Manfrius de Skun sighed. "You are more intelligent than we anticipated, Captain Hamilton. I am both delighted and alarmed. However, as the monitors have revealed, your stress factor is abnormally high. It is my decision that you should rest once more while we consider all the implications of your present condition."

"I'm doing fine, Dr. de Skun. I don't need to rest. All I want is —"

Abruptly sound and vision faded; and Idris was left alone momentarily with unexpressed thoughts. Then they, too, were engulfed by darkness. And there was nothing—not even dreams.

13

HE WOKE UP in his bunk. The cabin light was on. He looked at his hands. They were sweating, shaking.

There had been dreams. He remembered them. He remembered them vividly. Dreams! Such dreams!

Apprehensively, he felt his head. No scars, no wounds, no bandages. A normal head.

But in the dreams . . .

He did not want to think about them. He willed himself not to think about them.

Something was wrong. He did not want to think about that, either. But he had to think about it. The implications were enormous.

He should have been in a field of zero G.

He wasn't.

He moved carefully. All his limbs ached, felt strange, felt as they might feel if he had been drinking too much yet remained illusively sober. They felt abnormally heavy, heavier than they should feel on either Mars or Earth. Perhaps he had been ill.

That could be it.

He remembered that he had been near to breakdown before lift-off from Earth. He remembered his conversation with Orlando, the written authorisation that would enable Orlando to place him under restraint if, in Orlando's opinion, the captain had flipped.

Carefully, he got out of the bunk. The cabin seemed wrong. Something seemed wrong. But then probably something or everything would seem wrong if he really had fallen off his trolley.

His limbs ached abominably. Jesus Christ, why? Slowly, agonisingly, he made his way to the door. It was locked.

All very right and proper. It figured. If you have a mad captain on your hands, lock him up and throw away the key before he does something stupid, like wrecking the vessel. Especially if said captain had the wit to give you the necessary authority before he started picking daisies . . .

The last flowers of Earth . . .

Now why should that phrase come into his mind?

Idris Hamilton sat down on the chair by his desk, sweating, shaking. There was a whole heap of crazy notions tied up in a sack somewhere in a dark room in his head. He knew they were there, alive, struggling to get out. He didn't want them to get out. Because if they did, nothing would make sense any more.

He decided to use the intercom, talk to somebody— Orlando, Leo, Suzy. Any damn fool who would listen. There was a lot to tell them. The bloody nightmares, the grotesque thoughts, were busy cutting a hole in the sack. He didn't want to know about them. He really didn't. Pride stopped him from using the intercom. He might say things he would never want anyone to hear.

"But they are dead," he said aloud in a matter-of-fact voice. He had a sudden, dreadful vision of Orlando, choking, sucked out of the navigation deck into a wilderness of stars. "I am dead also."

Now he knew he was mad because, demonstrably, he was alive.

The mad can make their own laws. He decided to explore his madness.

"I am dead, and the *Dag Hammarskjold* was destroyed by sabotage. Also, I am alive and locked in the master's cabin. Also the *Dag* has touched down because I experience G."

The sack was torn open. Zylonia, Manfrius de Skun, the

74

planet Minerva, a brain in a life-support tank.

Not realities. Sick imaginings only. He bit his finger, felt the pain, saw the blood come.

No brain in a tank. The brain in Spain can't feel much pain . . .

And then he heard the cuckoo clock. He had been trying not to see it all the time. He had succeeded. He had not felt it was necessary to avoid hearing it. Even madness has its limitations.

But the cuckoo—lost bird of Earth—popped out twelve times and said "Cuckoo!"

And the bulkhead clock showed that it was indeed twelve o'clock.

Idris remembered his calculations—remembered everything—and screamed.

The cabin door opened. Zylonia came in.

Idris Hamilton fell backwards out of his chair, hit the bond-fuzz, curled up in the womb position and began to suck his thumb.

14

"CATATONIC SHOCK," SAID Manfrius de Skun. "It was our fault entirely. I must apologise. A miscalculation. I judged that you would probably adjust to the new situation better if you were allowed to be alone for a while. It was a bad mistake. I hope you will forgive me."

Idris lay in his bunk, not looking at Dr. de Skun, staring at the ceiling.

"I don't feel a thing," he said calmly. "I suppose you shot me full of happy juice."

"You are under sedation, yes. You will not need it much longer. You have a very resilient personality, Captain Hamilton. Or, if I may put it in a less clinical way, you are a brave man."

"Yes." Idris gave a weak laugh. "I screamed. I cried like a baby. That is a sign of courage?"

"Captain Hamilton, courage manifests itself in peculiar and divers ways. You have passed through the trauma of death, you endured a twilight existence as a brain in a life-support system, and your sanity has survived the transference of that brain to a new body. By any standards, a man who can survive multiple trauma of such magnitude is exceptionally courageous. If we had a hundred such as you on Minerva we would . . ." He stopped, confused.

"What would you do?"

"Nothing. Forgive me. I am tired. I talk stupidly. Since

your crisis, I have had little sleep."

Idris was silent for a while. Then he said: "It was the clock—the damned clock. It said 'Cuckoo!' twelve times, and the bulkhead clock showed the same time. And I blew my main circuits . . . Do you know what a cuckoo is?"

"A mythical bird of Mars," said Manfrius de Skun.

Idris laughed. "Wrong. A real bird of Earth."

Zylonia spoke. He had not been aware of her presence. "I am sorry about the clock, Idris. I left it in the cabin because I thought —"

"Because you thought it would remind me of a girl who took off her clothes for a brain in a tank. It did." He was still staring at the ceiling.

"Soon you will be well enough to meet people, to explore the Five Cities," she said brightly. "It must be wonderful to live normally again, to breathe and eat and —"

Again he cut her short. "Dr. de Skun, what happened to the previous tenant?"

"The previous tenant? Who are you talking about, captain?"

Idris tapped his head. "The guy who used to live between these cars. Have we simply exchanged apartments? Is he now stuck in my tank, trying to figure out what it is all about? Or did you just scoop him out of his skull and drop him in the trash can?" He laughed. "I have a more than passing interest. I understand we are closely related."

Manfrius de Skun sighed. "He is not in your tank, nor is he in the trash can. We are not murderers. As I have already told you, the brain in your cloned body was not allowed to mature or to achieve integrated self-consciousness."

"So, the poor bastard was still-born. But he is my brother. So you will understand that I am mildly curious as to his present whereabouts."

Again Dr. de Skun sighed. "You should not anthropomorphize. We are discussing not a personality but a brain that was never alive beyond the stimulation of its motor activities . . . However, it has been preserved in suspended animation."

"Liquid helium?"

"Yes, liquid helium."

"Why preserve it if it was never alive?"

"Captain Hamilton, there are several valid reasons why we should wish to preserve this brain. It is of immense historical, scientific and social value. The entire project, I believe, marks a turning point in our history and in our entire social structure." He smiled. "At this time, you are probably the most important person on the planet."

"I am glad you are preserving what is left of my brother," said Idris evenly. "Sometime, perhaps, you will be able to give him another body and lift him out of the mental twilight you had to keep him in."

"That is certainly not beyond the bounds of possibility," said Manfrius de Skun confidently.

"But then the process is infinite," went on Idris. "No matter how many times you pull the rabbit out of the hat, you are left with one brain minus a body."

Dr. de Skun was confused. "What does this mean—the rabbit out of the hat?"

"Sorry. An ancient metaphor. Traditionally, the classic trick for a conjuror—an illusionist—of Earth was to produce a living rabbit, a small furry quadruped, from a top hat." He saw the look of blankness on Manfrius de Skun's face and tried to explain further. "A top hat is—was—a kind of formal covering for the head. It was made of stiff cloth and looked like an inverted cooking pan with a wide brim and no handle."

"So?" Dr. de Skun still did not understand. "What is the significance of this furry terrestrial quadruped when we are discussing the question of cloned bodies?"

"Forget it. The meaning will become apparent in the course of time." Suddenly, Idris felt alive, very much alive. He felt like making use of the body that had been given him by Minervan science. He swung himself out of the bunk and faced Dr. de Skun and Zylonia. "Meanwhile, I am going to explore this world into which you have resurrected me."

"I do not think it is wise," said Dr. de Skun. "At the

moment, I do not think it is wise. Be patient. You have only just recovered from the transfer."

"Dr. de Skun, I have been waiting a long time. And I have run out of patience. Until you gave me this body, I depended on you totally. Now, I am relatively independent. I am in a position to make decisions."

"For the time being," said Manfrius de Skun, "I recommend—I forbid you to leave this room. We must be sure that you are fully recovered from the transplant before you enter the next phase."

Idris laughed. "Dr. de Skun, you are not now in a position to dictate. You presumed to play the role of Frankenstein, and you have created a monster capable of independent action. Don't ask me about Frankenstein, it would take too long . . . Do you have an army on this planet? Do you have men who are trained to kill?"

Manfrius de Skun threw up his hands in horror. "Captain Hamilton, we have lived in peace for thousands of years. Violence is abhorrent to us."

"Good. I win. I am not only a trained spaceman, Dr. de Skun, I have also been trained to kill—if necessary—with my bare hands. And violence is not totally abhorrent to me. So I am going out of this cabin—and *I* recommend that neither of you try to stop me. My brother's muscles seem almost as good as those I used to have."

His legs felt good. His body felt good. He felt good all over. He was alive again.

Zylonia said: "Please don't do anything stupid, Idris."

He ignored her. With sudden speed, he darted past her and Manfrius de Skun to the door. It opened easily.

He passed through the doorway and found himself in a large, bright room that looked vaguely like the traffic control centre of some large space-port. He took it all in at a glance. There were banks of monitor screens, a computer console, and a large number of young men and women. The Peeping Toms and Thomasinas who had doubtless monitored his existence in the tank and his reactions after being transferred to the cloned body. Clearly, also, they had witnessed his recent exchange with Manfrius de Skun.

Five rather solid-looking young men formed a semi-circle round the doorway.

"Please, Captain Hamilton," said one. "Dr. de Skun knows best. Please return to your cabin, and have patience."

He straightened the fingers of both hands, and imagined each hand to be made of steel, as he had been taught to do, long, long ago. He crouched into the attack position. "Gentlemen, it is my intention to pass," he said calmly.

Two of the young men came forward as if to crowd him back into the cabin. He chopped at the throat of one of them and almost simultaneously kicked the other in the stomach. They fell coughing, retching, groaning.

The other two retreated, with shocked expressions on their faces. There were cries of horror, and a girl technician screamed.

Zylonia rushed out of the cabin. "Idris, what have you done?"

He glanced at her warily, then at the two men on the floor. "They will be all right in a minute. It's shock, chiefly." He gave a faint smile. "I didn't hit them very hard." His glance flickered around the room. There were, perhaps, fifteen technicians—men and women. He couldn't take them all—particularly if a couple of bright young men had the wit to get behind him.

But since he had dealt so swiftly with two of those who had tried to force him back into the cabin, none of them seemed eager to come within reach. They were demoralised now; but presently they would start thinking again.

"These people have spent a great deal of time trying to help you," said Zylonia angrily. "This is how you repay them?"

"I thank them for their help," said Idris evenly. "I am immensely grateful for all the work they have done to ensure that I survived. But now that I am fully alive once more— no longer a prisoner in a nutrient tank—my freedom is precious, very precious. I wish to explore this world into which I have been reborn. If I am not hindered, no one will

80

come to any harm."

Manfrius de Skun emerged from the cabin. "Captain Hamilton, I beg you to reconsider. You have demonstrated that you are in full possession of your faculties and in total harmony with your new body. Allow us a little more time to determine whether your integration is temporary or permanent."

"Dr. de Skun, you should be very proud of your achievement. I am a man once more, capable of completely independent action. I assume this is what you wanted. Now I choose to exercise my freedom. Try to see it from my point of view. So far I have had to depend on information about Minerva from you and Zylonia. Now, I must see for myself. I want to find out about this world you have thrust me into, and I want to find out about the fate of the children who were my charges on the *Dag Hammarskjold*. For my own peace of mind, there can be no more delay."

Manfrius de Skun gave a deep sigh and shrugged. "You ignore my professional opinion, so it is on your own head. Zylonia, take him wherever he wishes to go. Show him whatever—or whoever—he wishes to see."

15

ABOVE ALL, IDRIS wanted to see the other survivors from the *Dag Hammarskjold*—the eleven children and one teacher whom the Minervans had managed to resuscitate. Until the *Dag* had been destroyed by the senseless and desperate sabotage of doomed Earthmen at Woomera, the children and their teachers had been regarded by Idris chiefly as the last, precious cultural and genetic cargo that could be lifted from the dying world. They had been taken aboard already encapsulated in their life-support systems. Each suspended animation unit was simply a priceless item on the ship's manifest.

He remembered looking at the titanium-clad suspended animation units and thinking of them as huge bombs—bombs of intelligence and initiative that would explode upon Mars and help to shape its future. The children, he knew, all had intelligence quotients of genius level. That was why they had been chosen. Primarily, he had regarded them as a cargo of super-brains — potential Newtons, Einsteins, Schweitzers who would leaven the intellectual development of the Martian élite and make invaluable contributions to the advancement of civilisation on the fourth planet.

But that was long ago—long, long ago. Now there were no Earthmen or Martians left. There were only Minervans, living in their synthetic grottoes on a frozen planet six billion miles from the sun.

So the children now were much more to him than super-brains. They were living time-machines, capable of transporting him across the black centuries of oblivion. Capable of reassuring him by bringing to life once more the ideas and attitudes—the very smell—of the Earth that had passed into history. Or so he thought . . .

The meeting he had demanded took place in Talbot Hall, in Talbot City. He was already becoming sick of hearing the name Talbot. But the memory of Garfield Talbot, the man who had settled the tenth planet, had achieved semi-divine status in Minervan culture. Garfield Talbot was the man who had assured the survival of mankind.

It was a strange event. Instead of the informal atmosphere that Idris had hoped for, the meeting had been deliberately organised for an audience. Besides Zylonia and Manfrius de Skun, nearly a hundred other Minervans were present.

Dr. de Skun seemed rather agitated, and Zylonia also looked tense. Idris guessed that the situation was now out of Dr. de Skun's control, and felt a twinge of regret at having forced his hand. Dr. de Skun was, after all, responsible for resuscitating Idris and providing him with a new body. The least he could have done in return, perhaps, would have been to exercise a little more patience and to have allowed the doctor to play it his way. But there was no going back. Having made his 'break-out'—the news of which must have spread very rapidly in this small community—Idris was determined to retain the initiative. If he capitulated now, he felt, he would reduce himself to the status of laboratory animal.

Before the Earth children and their surviving teacher were produced, Idris faced a number of questions from the Minervans. These questions were invited somewhat hesitantly by Manfrius de Skun.

"Ladies and gentlemen, you are all familiar with Captain Hamilton's history. As you see, he is completely in harmony with his new body." Dr. de Skun gave a nervous laugh. "Indeed, he adjusted to it far more rapidly than was anticipated, and there are those among us who have good reason to believe that his co-ordination is at optimum performance." That, no doubt, was a reference to his emergence from the cabin that was supposed to be his psychological womb. It was received in frigid silence. "The point is," went on Dr. de Skun desperately, "that Captain Hamilton is once more a totally integrated person—integrated, that is, within the framework of his own cultural attitudes. How he will respond to Minervan culture cannot, of course, yet be determined. But, in a sense, that is irrelevant. His presence among you justifies the techniques of transplant that we have been trying to establish for so long. He has demonstrated that a form of immortality is now within our grasp. To that extent he is our benefactor.

"His present overwhelming desire is to meet the surviving children of Earth that it was his mission to transport to Mars some five thousand years ago. He will meet them presently. Meanwhile, I am sure he will be kind enough to answer any questions you may care to ask."

There was a short silence. Then someone said: "Captain Hamilton, do you feel that after such traumatic experience you can be wholly sane?"

Idris shrugged. "Define sanity, and perhaps I can answer the question . . . I feel that I am in full possession of my clone brother's faculties. I understand my situation, I try hard to accept it, and I believe I make rational responses. To that extent, I think that I am reasonably sane."

"Was it a sane act to attack technicians of the team responsible for your resuscitation?"

"My environment seemed claustrophobic. Which of you has endured what I have endured? None. Therefore, I think, you cannot understand my motivations. I did not wantonly attack the technicians. They barred my way. They attempted to restrain me. Rightly or wrongly, I could not accept that restraint."

"Captain Hamilton." This time it was a woman who spoke. "What do you think of the women of Minerva?"

He smiled and glanced at Zylonia. "Apart from Miss de Herrens, I have had no contact with the women of Minerva.

If she is typical then I do not think I shall have cause to complain."

"Is it true that while your brain was still in the life-support system, you required her to disrobe?"

"It is true."

"Why was that?"

"I did not have a body. She did. I wanted to see it, to know what it was like. I wanted to observe all its movements and functions. And, apart from the obvious sexual motivation, I thought that it might help to keep me sane." Out of the corner of his eye, he saw that Manfrius de Skun was getting even more nervous.

"You felt you were in danger of becoming insane?" Another voice. A male voice. The question was deceptively gentle. From Dr. de Skun's agitated reaction, Idris sensed that the question was not so harmless as it appeared. He wondered why. He wondered how best to counter it. Finally he decided that the best way was by absolute honesty.

"Of course, I thought I might become insane."

There was an almost unified gasp from the audience.

"Consider the facts, ladies and gentlemen," he went on calmly. "I was a brain in a life-support system. I had learned that I had died in space five thousand years before, that my brain had been salvaged and resuscitated by techniques at which I can only marvel, and that I was on the outermost planet of the solar system. Consider also that I had no means of checking any data given to me. Under the circumstances, it would surely have been an indication of madness if I failed to doubt my own sanity." There was some nervous and appreciative laughter. "But," he concluded, "I believe that a normal Minervan brain, suitably prepared beforehand, would not be subjected to the stresses which I had to face. A Minervan brain, I am convinced, could be transferred from body to support system and back to body without experiencing any stress that would imperil sanity." He glanced at Dr. de Skun, who seemed now a little more relaxed. "I am sure," he added evenly, "that what Dr. de Skun has discovered during the course of my resuscitation can ultimately be of benefit to you all. Needless to say, he and his team have my profound gratitude."

There was a short burst of applause. Idris noted the gratitude in Manfrius de Skun's eyes and in Zylonia's, and knew that he had said the right things.

"Another question, please."

"Let it be the last, then," said Manfrius de Skun, his voice authoritative once more. "Captain Hamilton has been most co-operative."

"Captain Hamilton, now that you are fully restored to life, what would you like to do with all the useful time that is now ahead of you?"

He smiled. "Well, you already know my immediate objective. After that I want to spend some time finding out about you Minervans. I am told that, unlike Earth and Mars, you have succeeded in developing a stable culture. I want to find out all I can about it." He paused. "But, in the long term I have one overwhelming ambition. I am a spaceman. You have space flight. I want to mount an expedition to Earth."

There was a deathly silence. The good will that seemed to have been building up suddenly evaporated. The Minervans stared at him with expressionless faces. He was amazed.

"I think," said Manfrius de Skun hurriedly, "you will all appreciate that Captain Hamilton knows little or nothing of Minervan values. He cannot be expected to appreciate our attitudes until he has had time to explore our society."

"He is tainted!" said a woman's voice, shrilly. "He attacked two of the project group, and now he wants to go back to that planet. He is tainted."

There were murmurs of approval. Idris was aware of a sudden, chilling hostility.

"The E-people are ready and waiting," said Zylonia in a voice that shook somewhat. "Captain Hamilton has endured much. Let us ensure that this encounter with the children he tried so valiantly to take to Mars is a pleasant one."

16

IDRIS EXPECTED TO meet children. Instead he was confronted by young men and women. At first he thought he was being tricked, and said so. But Dr. de Skun explained what had happened.

"Captain Hamilton, your abrupt rejection of our programme of psychological adjustment has given us no opportunity to prepare you to face certain facts which must now be made apparent. Minerva takes nearly five hundred Earth years to complete one orbit of the sun. To try to reckon personal time in Minervan years would be meaningless. Therefore we have retained Martian time. As you know, the Martian year is almost two Earth years. The wreckage of the *Dag Hammarskjold* was salvaged eighteen M-years ago. I and my team began work upon the resuscitation and rehabilitation of your brain almost immediately. But there was much arduous preparation, including the development of special equipment, and much testing before we could be reasonably certain that we could restore your brain and the personality encoded in it to a normal function. It was only when we were sure that this would be the case that we began resuscitation procedures upon the children. That was four M-years ago. Since there was no need to provide artificial life-support systems for their brains, the task proceeded relatively quickly. We have had great success. Six of the children and their teacher are now fully in possession of their faculties and integrated to our Minervan society. Judge for yourself."

Idris, gazing at the twelve people now confronting him, silently worked out a few simple sums. He had been brought to Minerva eighteen M-years ago, which was roughly thirty-four E-years ago. And the children, therefore, had been restored to life just over seven E-years ago. That figured. According to the manifest, the children he had taken on board at Woomera were eleven to twelve years of age. Now they would be eighteen or nineteen, Earth time. It figured.

He spoke in English. It was hard to speak in English. He had become so accustomed to speaking—even thinking—in Minervan.

"Please nod your heads slightly if you can understand what I say. I know that you are of varied nationalities, but I assume that most of you will have some acquaintance with my native tongue. I assume also that all of you are familiar with the Minervan language, as I am. We will use it presently; but for the moment, I would like to preserve some degree of privacy."

Six of them and the woman who was obviously the teacher nodded their heads. The remaining five looked at him blankly. Among the six was a negro boy, an Indian or Pakistani girl and a girl who seemed to be of Chinese origin.

"It would be more helpful, Idris, if you were to talk to them in Minervan," said Zylonia.

"I will be helpful presently," he retorted, also in Minervan. "Meanwhile, I wish to exchange a few semi-private words with these people for whose safety I was once responsible."

"Captain Hamilton." It was the teacher speaking. Her hair was white, Idris noted. Yet she could only be in her late twenties or early thirties—Earth time. He tried to remember the details of the manifest, but could not.

"Captain Hamilton, I do not think we should antagonize our hosts. My name is Mary Evans. I am, as you probably know, the surviving teacher." She spoke in English, with a pleasing Welsh lilt that sounded entirely marvellous.

"Well, Miss Evans, may I say that your voice is like music to my ears. I have no intention of antagonizing our hosts, as you put it. Indeed, I have every reason to be grateful to them—so far. But I have been somewhat isolated —no doubt you know the facts—and I want to get one or two things clear in my mind. Have the Minervans treated you well? Have they tried to brainwash you or restrict you or compel you in any way?"

Mary Evans smiled. "Captain Hamilton, you are very suspicious, perhaps rightly so. I think I can speak for all of us when I say we are filled with gratitude for what the Minervans have done. Truly, there has been no compulsion of any kind."

"So you will be content to spend the rest of your days here?"

She sighed. "There is no choice . . . Let me give you some advice. You are a brave man. We all know what you have endured. But try to adjust to their philosophy. It is for the best."

"Your hair is white, yet you have a young face."

"I am now thirty-four Earth years old," said Mary. "Perhaps the shock of being resuscitated on the wrong planet accounts for the white hair . . . Be at ease, Captain Hamilton. The Minervans are not sinister. They have been very good to us. Ask any of the children." She grinned. "If we can still call them children. They are men and women, I suppose. And they have adapted very well."

He turned to a dark-haired, dark-skinned and quite beautiful girl—the one who was either Indian or Pakistani. "What is your name?"

"Annali Prodoski, sir."

"You need not say sir, Annali."

"It is a mark of respect only, Captain Hamilton. You tried so hard to get us to Mars, and we are very grateful."

"Do you like living here on Minerva?"

She shrugged. "Mars would have been better. But the Minervans are very kind."

"Have you been out on the surface?"

"No. There is no need. Conditions are very difficult up there, and special training is necessary. Even in a space-suit it is possible to drown in a hydrogen lake. I think —"

"Have you ever wanted to get away from this subterranean life, to go up top and see what it is really like?"

"Yes, but it really is too dangerous."

"Who says so?"

"The Minervans. Very few of them go to the surface or want to go to the surface. Of course, there are scientists and space engineers who must work out there, and —"

Again he interrupted her. "Annali, do you want to spend the rest of your life in an underground city on a frozen planet six billion miles from the sun?"

Annali Prodoski seemed confused. "When you put it like that, it does not seem a very pleasant prospect. But we have no choice. There is nothing else we can do, is there?"

"There might be," he said enigmatically.

All the time that he had been speaking in English, Idris had sensed a growing unrest among the Minervans present. He knew that Zylonia and Manfrius de Skun would be able to follow his conversation; but from the blank and hostile looks on the faces of the rest, it was evident that they had no familiarity with a language that had been dead for five thousand years.

He looked at Zylonia and Dr. de Skun, both plainly unhappy at the way things were turning out. There was an atmosphere of tension and hostility among the other Minervans that puzzled him greatly. Well, he would think about that later. Now was the time to take some of the heat out, if at all possible.

He continued his questioning of the Earth children in the Minervan tongue. The tension diminished; but much of the hostility remained.

The responses he got from the children who had once been entrusted to his care were startlingly similar. They were all filled with gratitude for what the Minervans had done. They now thought of themselves not as Earth people but as Minervan citizens. And they seemed content to

90

spend the rest of their days in the underground cities of this desolate world without ever feeling the need to go out on to the surface and explore.

He was surprised that children of genius level should accept the situation so docilely and should be apparently devoid of curiosity. This, of course, was understandable in the case of those suffering from brain damage. He questioned them carefully—in Minervan. Apart from a Russian boy, Alexei Bolkonski, who had a serious speech defect, the rest were able to answer him rationally. One of them, Natalie van Doren, an American, curiously enough had retained her high intelligence quotient but could not remember anything of her life before she had been resuscitated on Minerva. The remaining three with brain damage had lost their paranormal intelligence but were by no means reduced to the level of cabbages. Their reactions were slow, they needed time to formulate their thoughts; but they got there in the end.

All the children and their teacher, Idris discovered, had integrated well into Minervan culture. Several of them had become involved in scientific projects. Mary Evans, naturally enough, was a specialist in Terran history. Even Alexei Bolkonski held an important post in a new hydroponics project.

Presently, Idris tired of this public ecounter. Later, he decided, he would seek out these children—no, he must no longer think of them as children—these people, privately, and try to get behind the masks they apparently displayed for the Minervans. Then, perhaps, he would discover what they really thought and felt.

The interview came to an end. Dr. de Skun seemed relieved. So did Zylonia. So did the Earth children and Mary Evans. In fact, the only person who seemed neither relieved nor satisfied was Idris Hamilton. And he, as he knew, was simply exhausted. The marriage between old brain and new body was a good one. But like all marriages, it needed time to adjust.

17

HE WOULD NOT go back to the simulated master's cabin of
the *Dag Hammarskjold*. Where else was there for him to go?
Answer: to the home of Zylonia de Herrens, the woman
with whom he had lived—if only in the spiritual sense—
since his resurrection. The woman who had stripped for
him, who had shit and peed for him, who had eaten for him
and moved gracefully for him when he was nothing more
than a sentient thing—a few pounds of cells in a nutrient
solution.

The home of Zylonia de Herrens . . .

A splendid place. A small room, with a minute kitchen,
and an even smaller bathroom, all hollowed out from rock
twenty metres below the surface of Minerva, along a broad,
well-lit corridor grandly designated Eastern Avenue, Talbot
City. Apartment Ninety-One.

It was comfortable, at least. Maximum use had been
made of available space. There was a service wall with a
small push-button control console. It concealed extensible
furniture—a bed, a table, extra chairs. It also contained a
large tri-di screen, a V-phone, a tape-deck and library and
a drinks' cabinet. The wall opposite the door was apparently
a large picture window looking out on to an immense garden
where non-existent flowers, shrubs and strange grasses
matured, bloomed, withered and died. An electronic illusion, but a pleasing electronic illusion. The kind that was

necessary to keep a subterranean race sane.

The wall opposite the service panel was covered by a large curtain. Zylonia touched a button and the curtain rolled back to reveal the glass wall of a fantastic aquarium. It was breathtakingly beautiful. In it were brilliant corals, multi-coloured fish, lobsters, crabs, eels, minute forests of sea-weed and a bed of golden sand.

Idris was astounded, fascinated. He felt he could gaze at it for hours. Here were recognisable creatures of Earth, six billion miles away from their parent planet, swimming about unconcerned in an ideal environment.

"You see," said Zylonia, "we may live on a frozen world, but we have created for ourselves an environment that fulfils human needs. Would you like a drink?"

"What kind of a drink?" he enquired cautiously.

"Scotch, gin, kafra. White wine or red wine."

"You produce all these on Minerva?"

"We cannot import them, Idris."

"Yes, stupid of me. I'm tired. What is kafra?"

"Martian brandy. I thought you would have been familiar with it."

"No. Evidently it was after my time. But I'll try it. Brandy is brandy is brandy."

"That is a strange remark."

"I paraphrase an ancient Earth writer called Gertrude Stein."

She poured the drink. "Forgive me. I do not understand the significance."

"Nor do I, to tell the truth." He drank and savoured the warmth in his throat. "But brandy still tastes reasonably like brandy . . . Are you married, Zylonia? Do you have one man only whom you love and with whom you make love? It is one of the questions I should have asked some time ago."

She smiled. "We do not have permanent one to one relationships. They make for jealousy and possessiveness. At the moment, I am unattached." She hesitated. "The project has taken too much of my time and energy for me to be able to respond to sexual stimulus."

"That is a cold way of putting it."

"I am a scientist. It is an accurate evaluation, I think."

He emptied his glass. "This kafra is no match for a good French brandy." He gave a grim laugh. "But I know that I shall drink no more French brandy; and truly I realise, therefore, that I am in a new Dark Age. May I have another?"

Zylonia refilled his glass and poured one for herself. "You make jokes. Thas is good. A sign of integration... Do you wish to get drunk?"

"Possibly. I am not entirely used to having a new body. Perhaps I should test its limits of endurance—in a scientific way, of course . . . What kind of toast do you make on Minerva when you drink with a friend?"

"We say: Talbot lives."

"I have a better toast."

"What is that?"

"Earth lives." He held up his glass. "Will you drink to that?"

"Why not? Earth lives."

They touched glasses and drank.

"What about children?" said Idris abruptly. "You have to have a one to one relationship to rear children. Or am I being quaint?"

She laughed. "You are being splendidly quaint. The nuclear family is prehistoric. Psycho-historically, it provided the roots for tribalism, nationalism, chauvinism, sectarianism —in short it created a violent and unstable society."

"Jesus Christ!" he exploded. "I have a hell of a lot to learn about you Minervans."

"Are you a Christian?" she asked. "My researches show that the Christian countries of Earth were very aggressive and brutal."

"No, I am not a Christian . . . If the nuclear family, as you call it, is now obsolete what have you Minervans replaced it with?"

"Our mating criterion is based simply on genetic improve-

94

ment. Every woman who is approved by the Department of Genetics has the right to bear two children by approved male donors. In some cases, women with exceptional genetic qualities may bear three children or allow their fertilized ova to be implanted in a suitable host."

"May I have another shot of kafra?"

Zylonia said: "So you do intend to get drunk. Help yourself, Idris. It is a pity, but I understand. I think that what I have said shocks you. Is that not so?"

Idris poured himself a large one. A very large one. "I name this drink the Hamilton cup. It is to be taken in one swallow." He drained the glass and laughed. "Hereafter let all Earthmen who touch down on Minerva take the Hamilton cup as I once took the Gagarin cup."

"Are you already drunk?"

"No, I am not already drunk . . . Are we monitored?"

She looked genuinely surprised. "No. Why should we be? This is my home. You are my guest."

"Good. Then, dear Zylonia, I can tell you that your Minervan culture stinks. It stinks of computers, it stinks of that latter day Jesus, Garfield Talbot, and it stinks of scientific dictatorship."

"You *are* drunk."

He poured himself another. "Correction. I am only beginning to be drunk. Give me a little time."

Zylonia stood up. "I think I should call Dr. de Skun."

"Don't try to call anyone, Zylonia. You have seen me in action. I am not yet that drunk."

"You would threaten me?" There was anger in her voice. "I have been trying very hard to believe that you are not a violent man."

He gave a great sigh. "I am sorry. I apologise. Call Dr. de Skun if you want to . . . I just wish you wouldn't, that's all."

"Very well, I will not call him yet. Now listen to me carefully, Idris. I have some imagination, and I have considerable knowledge of you. I know, for example, how you feel about Suzy and the other members of your crew. I know something of your childhood, and I even know about the significance of the Gagarin cup, and the pride you take in the fact that it was offered to you by a great Earth hero. It is all in your psycho-history . . . So I have some idea of the feelings of isolation and loneliness you feel, and of the suspicions and anxieties you entertain. But please proceed very cautiously, for your sake and for ours."

He made as if to speak, but she silenced him with a gesture. "No, hear me out, please. Then I will listen to what you have to say. That is fair, is it not?"

"That is fair," he agreed. "May I have one last shot of this kafra? It's not bad once you stop trying to compare it with a real brandy."

She shrugged. "Help yourself. If you choose to use alcohol as a barrier against unpleasant realities, I am sad. But I will not stop you. However, before you become incapable of thinking, there are some things I must tell you. You know that we have worked very hard—Dr. de Skun especially—to restore you to full life. You know also that, because of the success we have achieved, the prospect of immortality, or, at least, a greatly extended life span, seems within the grasp of ordinary Minervan citizens. With the cloning technique and brain transplant, there seems to be no theoretical reason why a person should not live as long as his brain is capable of accepting and storing data, of making rational decisions, of carrying out motor responses, and of maintaining the body he occupies. What you do not know, I think, is that this project is a matter of controversy. That is why, now that the technique has been proved to be physically possible, your subsequent behaviour is of the utmost importance."

"I don't see why. Whatever I do now cannot affect Dr. de Skun's achievement."

She sighed. "It can. Believe me it can. There are many Minervans who would dearly wish to have you declared insane."

"What purpose would that serve?"

"It would block the project. They would be able to claim

96

that the trauma of a brain transplant unhinges the reason. There are people who believe that it is unnatural and immoral to extend life beyond the limits imposed by nature."

Idris laughed. "I do not see that you have much of a problem. Presumably, if your purists get cancer or heart disease or even appendicitis, they will not accept surgery and so they will die off."

"It is not as simple as that. Approved surgical techniques —that is techniques established before Garfield Talbot led the exodus from Mars—are acceptable to the purists, as you call them. But the Triple-T party view with suspicion anything that has been developed since."

"What does Triple-T stand for?"

"True to Talbot . . . These people believe that our life on Minerva was meant as a form of expiation for the sins of mankind. Among the non-scientific sections of society they have strong support. The problem is made more acute by the fact that our life-expectancy is declining sharply. When Garfield Talbot colonised Minerva, the average person could expect to live about fifty M-years. Now the expectation has fallen to thirty-five M-years. Projections show that it will continue to shorten."

"Surely then, everyone should be happy about the success of brain transplant?"

Zylonia shook her head. "Not the Triple-T. They see the shortening of individual life as a form of punishment. They believe that only when we have discovered the correct way of life will the life-span increase. And then, they believe, immortality will develop naturally."

Idris was vastly amused. "So, after five thousand years, the human race—what is left of it—is still bedevilled by nut cases. *Plus ça change* . . . May I live with you, Zylonia? For a time, at least. I am not going back to that beautifully rigged mausoleum of the master's cabin on the *Dag*."

"You may live with me—for a time—if you behave yourself. But I shall have to report on your behaviour, you understand."

"That went without saying . . . May I also make love to

you?"

"Is it important that you should?"

"I think so."

She gave a faint smile. "Then, in the interests of scientific research, I have no objection."

"You will report my responses, naturally."

She gave him an impish look. "That, surely, is at the discretion of the investigator."

"Very fair . . . Shall we go to bed?"

"Were you always so direct?"

"Never. It is a new experience. I like it."

"Very well, Idris. We have already made love to each other in our minds, as you know. Perhaps it will be therapeutic for you if we accomplish it physically."

"Most therapeutic," he assured her. "Which damn button do I press to get the bed out of the wall?"

She showed him. When he turned to look at her again, she was already naked.

"This I like."

"This I think I will like also," she said. "But, afterwards, whether we are good or bad together, there is something I want you to do for me."

"What is it?"

"You will read a book. It is called *Talbot's Creed*. You promise to do this?"

"I promise." He took her in his arms and kissed her. She felt wonderful. She felt like a woman it was worth waiting five thousand years for.

18

ZYLONIA DE HERRENS was strange and fascinating. It was not until he had held her close to him physically as well as mentally that he realised quite how strange and how fascinating. He realised then that no man could ever hope to know what a woman was like unless he had been fully intimate with her. Not intimate just in the sense of taking her to bed; but intimate in the sense of exploring the range of implications and emotions involved in taking her to bed.

The first time he made love to her it was a kind of rape. He knew it, and so did she. The love play was brutal, insistent, direct, fierce. Idris was surprised at his own ruthlessness, at his apparent disregard when she protested, pleaded, struggled. He held her roughly, taking pleasure in hearing the moans and outraged grunts as he thrust into her repeatedly, as if she alone should be punished, as if she alone were responsible for all that he had endured.

"I haven't made love for five thousand years!" he shouted at her wildly. "You clever ones have brought a primitive savage back from the dead. So you can't complain if his manners are a little different from those of the antiseptic lads on Minerva."

Then he held her breast tightly with one hand until she groaned in pain and anger, until he felt her whole body become tense upon the brink of orgasm. Then he stared at her eyes, as if looking for some kind of message, and let

the semen pulse out of his body and into hers in slow excruciating surges that seemed as if they would never end.

"Earth lives!" he shouted, gloating upon the now glazed
look in her eyes, the slack open mouth, the tongue that pro-
truded almost as if Zylonia were being strangled.

"Earth lives!" he shouted.

Her body stiffened. She cried aloud in pain, wonderment,
acceptance, ecstasy. Then all her flesh became soft, relaxed,
and she uttered a deep sigh. Idris let himself lie upon her
very lightly. With great tenderness, he kissed her lips and
her forehead. Then, tenderly, he began to stroke her hair.

For a time there was silence. For a time there was nothing
to say. The sweat of their bodies mingled. There was the
sweet, subtle odour of fulfilment about them.

At length, Zylonia said: "No man has ever done such
things to me before." She said it not by way of complaint
or reproach, but in sheer amazement.

Idris laughed. "You were not a virgin."

"No. I have made love with a number of men."

"And none of them did to you what I have done . . .
Therefore I should not be jealous, because I am the first."

"You are a strange person, Idris. You behaved like an
animal."

"I am an animal. I am an animal first, and an Earth man
second, and a civilised human being third . . . Anyway, how
would you know how an animal behaves?"

She smiled. "You have much to learn about Minerva. We
have farms. Ducks, geese, chickens, cows, bulls. I know how
animals behave. I worked on a farm during my first year in
psychology."

Idris could not restrain his laughter. "Farms! For you a
farm is a large man-made cave. I can remember farms that
stretched for hundreds of kilometres north and west under
the open sky. I can remember rain-drenched sheep grazing
on wet grass. I can even remember rare times of sunlight
and starlight. What do you know about farms?"

"Our farms," she said, "are in perfect ecological balance
under perfect climatic conditions—which is more, I think—

100

than your farms were. They produce exactly what is required. There is never a surplus, never a deficit. Which is more than can be said for the farms of Earth." She laughed. "So, primitive Earth man, prehistoric animal that you are, do not feel too superior . . . Well, you have at least demonstrated that you can make love in a violent and possessive fashion. What would you like to do next? Do you want —"

"Did you like it, the love-making?"

Her forehead wrinkled. "I don't know. It was shattering and painful. I don't know. My reactions are confused. Psychologically, that is interesting."

Idris kissed her. "The hell with psychology. Let's have the playback."

19

TALBOT'S CREED WAS a strange, intense book. Written three thousand Earth years ago, it embodied the idea and ideals of the strange, intense man who had written it. As he read, Idris began to comprehend some of the pressures under which scientists like Manfrius de Skun worked.

Garfield Talbot had been a man of extremes—a living paradox. He had been an autocrat who gave lip-service to democracy, a pacifist who could ruthlessly blast out of space a vessel whose captain refused to colonise Minerva, a religious fanatic who was also a kind of Utopian communist, a man who hated the very science that enabled him to colonise a frozen planet six billion miles from the sun.

On the one hand, he believed that every human being had a God-given right to determine his own destiny: on the other hand, he regarded himself as being divinely chosen to lead the remnants of mankind towards a new era of spiritual grace.

Garfield Talbot was 'democratically' elected to be the first president of the first Five Cities Council. Theoretically, he took advice from his fellow councillors. Theoretically decisions were arrived at by a voting process. In practice, Talbot was an absolute ruler, a beneficent despot.

He had a larger-than-life personality, an almost mystical aura. Men were afraid of him, women were fascinated by him. During his long and active career, he sired—or

102

acknowledged that he sired—fourteen children by eight women. Later, Idris learned that there were numerous people claiming direct patrilinear descent from Garfield Talbot in all the Five Cities. Most of them, not unnaturally, were the hard core of the Triple T party.

Part of Talbot's attraction lay in the fact that he was incorruptible. He wanted nothing for himself—except power. He wore the tunic of a hydroponics labourer; lived in a small room that contained little but a cooking stove, a table and a a bed; touched no alcoholic drinks and ate sparingly of the simplest foods.

He was, thought Idris, a sort of combination of Rasputin, Adolf Hitler and Mahatma Ghandi. If he had lived on Earth in the nineteenth or the twentieth century, he would undoubtedly have made himself master of a continent at the very least.

But he had led the exodus from a doomed Mars and made himself master of the colony he had established on this frozen planet at the perimeter of the solar system. Proportionally, his achievement was comparable to those of Alexander, Julius Caesar, Napoleon. Perhaps it was greater, because *Talbot's Creed* had survived as a political force for three thousand years.

There was no monetary system on Minerva. Talbot's simple Utopianism had seen to that. Money, he believed, was a corrupting influence. It caused men to work not for the common good but for the material advantages that money would buy. Neither was there any ownership of property, apart from personal possessions. There were no laws of inheritance, and there were no privileges of birth. Even Talbot's own children had been treated the same as all other children in the then small community—that is to say, when they were weaned they were taken to the communal crèche and given finally and absolutely to the care of surrogate mothers who were themselves trained nurses and teachers.

Perhaps the most significant of Talbot's achievements was his ruthless abolition of the one-to-one relationship known as marriage. It had been a matter of necessity. His small fleet of space ships had touched down on Minerva with a total complement of two hundred and twenty-three men and one hundred and fifty-eight women. If he had allowed the concept of marriage to remain, he would have had internecine strife on his hands within a couple of M-years. But promiscuity was not an acceptable alternative. That would simply bring emotional chaos.

Instead he hit upon the idea of time-pairing. The minimum time-pairing was for thirty days, covering one full ovulation cycle, in case the woman wished to conceive. The maximum period was one M-year, to accommodate those who desired at least a semi-permanent relationship. But, for obvious reasons, M-year pairings were discouraged among all except the intellectual or genetic élite.

Talbot's great obsession was with the notion of atonement and with what he called 'the rediscovery of the truly human nature'. The two ideas were permanently linked in his mind. This man, a mass of paradoxes, did not believe in a Christian God or in any godhead having its origins in terrestrial mythology. But he had an unshakable belief in Divine Purpose, in a disembodied and pure spiritual force responsible for the creation of sentient life throughout the cosmos.

Divine Purpose, he believed, had been affronted by man's misuse of science and technology. Divine Purpose had therefore visited dreadful destruction upon the civilisations of Earth and Mars. Divine Purpose could now best be served by the creation of a stable culture, free from greed, possessiveness, self-aggrandisement and all the corruption associated with the dead cultures of Earth and Mars.

For reasons never fully explained in the *Creed*, he hit upon the figure of ten thousand as being the maximum permissible population until mankind had discovered how to control or eliminate its baser instincts. So pairing required a licence and conception required a licence. And, while he lived, Garfield Talbot was the one person who ultimately decided whether a woman should be allowed to sleep for any length of time with a man, and when and by whom she should be allowed to conceive.

His mistrust of science—the science that, as he saw it, had been directly responsible for the destruction of life on two planets—was pathological. If he could have declared a moratorium on scientific research, he would have done so. But he was not quite strong enough for that. Many of the men and women he had brought from Mars were first-rank scientists who also mistrusted the purposes to which their work would be put. But they were more rational in their misgivings than Garfield Talbot.

He wanted science to stand still—to provide only the processes and techniques necessary for survival on Minerva. No more. They wanted science to develop in a way that would improve the quality of life. Inevitably, there was conflict.

One of the first major disagreements concerned the establishment of a city on the surface of Minerva. A number of engineers and physicists and a psychologist claimed that underground existence was unnecessary and might well be socially harmful. They drew up plans for dome colonies that could be built and extended for a fraction of the effort needed to construct underground accommodation. The psychologist maintained that living underground would, in the long term, produce a fear of open spaces that might ultimately restrict the Minervans to a subterranean existence for ever.

Garfield Talbot disapproved of the development of surface colonies for the very reasons that the project was advocated. He wanted the colonists to be restricted in their activities and in their attitudes. It was all part of his vague notion of racial atonement. Men must be discouraged from physical expansion so that they could concentrate on spiritual development. Basically, he saw the underground colonies as a kind of self-imposed prison settlement from which men would emerge only when they had purified themselves by contemplation and had come to terms with the aggressive instincts that had destroyed the cultures of Earth and Mars.

Nevertheless, the Surface Party had gained strength and some support, even from many who did not wish to go with them. In the end, Talbot had to allow the Surface Party to proceed with their plans. He made one stipulation: they could take with them enough equipment, fuel and food supplies to sustain them for half an M-year. After that, they must be self-reliant.

It seemed a fair decision. Except that Garfield Talbot instinctively knew that without strong leadership the project was doomed to failure.

He was right. The surface of Minerva was no place to attempt to carry out engineering projects according to democratic processes. The Surface Party, rejoicing in their new-found personal freedom, spent too much precious time and used up too much precious oxygen prospecting for suitable sites and engaging in democratic discussion to get the first accommodation dome and its vital hydroponics unit entirely self-supporting before supplies became critical.

They radioed Talbot City, then the only subterranean city in existence, asking for more fuel, more food, more equipment. Garfield Talbot refused, reminding them of the terms of the agreement and pointing out that the materials they had already used had severely restricted the programme of expansion for Talbot City and the corresponding increase of population.

The condition of the Surface Party became desperate. There were many casualties—chiefly from explosive decompression in worn-out space suits. Finally, they offered to abandon the project entirely if they were allowed to return to the subterranean refuge. Again Talbot refused. He argued that if they were prepared to break the terms of one agreement, they would be capable of breaking the terms of another. There could be no guarantee that, if they returned to Talbot City, once they had recovered themselves they would not again make demands for precious supplies to pursue an impossible project.

Eventually, in desperation, the survivors attempted to force their way back underground. There were, at the time, only four access air-locks for Talbot City. At each of these, several of Garfield Talbot's most trusted men were stationed. They were equipped with laser rifles. As the remnants of the

Surface Party attacked one of the air-locks with cutting equipment, half a dozen of Talbot's men emerged from another air-lock and took them in the rear. They were burned ruthlessly. There were no survivors.

As Idris read the *Creed*—a document of almost embarrassing honesty and self-revelation—he became fascinated by the psychological complexity of its author. Although Garfield Talbot was the kind of man who could blast a rebellious space-ship out of existence and mercilessly destroy dissident colonists, he was also the kind of man who could cheerfully go on half-rations—as he had done when a serious fault developed in one of the hydroponics systems—so that babies, pregnant women and children would not be deprived of nutrient.

Without him, Idris realised, the colony on Minerva would never have survived. With him, it had survived to achieve his ideal—the stable population of ten thousand. But his attitudes and philosophy had, over the centuries, become an inhibiting factor. The ghost of Garfield Talbot held the Minervans in thrall, stopped them from expanding, developing, evolving.

Now, Idris began to understand the courage of Manfrius de Skun and Zylonia. Now he had found a purpose in this, his second life.

The purpose was exorcism. The rigid beliefs of Garfield Talbot had dominated what was left of mankind too long.

20

DESPITE HIS GROWING involvement with Zylonia, Idris never forgot that she was an officer of the Mental Health Department, a member of the team that, having resuscitated him, were dedicated to studying and analysing his behaviour.

He was not just a man who had been given a new life and a new body. He was now, he realised, an important factor in Minervan politics. Upon his behaviour the success or failure of the immortality project would depend. He already knew that the Triple-T party would like him to be declared insane. They would be looking for any aspect of his behaviour that, according to Minervan standards, could be held to be totally irrational.

Having read *Talbot's Creed,* he had a very good idea of what was expected of him by orthodox Minervans. He would have to be very careful for a time in what he said and did.

On the other hand, it seemed reasonable to suppose that Zylonia, Manfrius de Skun and persons unknown were—temporarily, at least, on his side. They would probably go to great lengths to safeguard his interests and so preserve their immortality project. But would they be so friendly if they realised his true intentions? Idris doubted it. If they realised that he intended to do his best to break the psychological stranglehold of Minervan tradition they, too, would probably regret that he had been successfully resuscitated.

Therefore he counselled himself to caution and to patience. So far as he knew, the Minervans had one serviceable interplanetary space-ship. The Minervans already knew that he wanted to go back to Earth. That alone, in their eyes, was a heretical or insane desire. What they must not suspect was that, sooner or later, he intended to steal the *Amazonia*. If he could recruit people to help him, so much the better. But if not, then, by God, he would lift off single-handed, somehow, and make the Earth shoot alone.

Earth . . . After five thousand years some of the crap brought about by mankind's rape of the planet must have cleared. With no more internal combustion engines, with no more atomic energy plants to supply the insatiable energy demands of the teeming millions, with no more chemicals poured lethally over the fertile soil, something must have survived. Earth was too old, too big, too strong to be totally destroyed by man. Something must have survived. The oceans that gave birth to life could not have entirely died. Nor, indeed, could all land life have been wiped out. Life was infinitely persistent, infinitely adaptable.

Having destroyed their own environment as did the dinosaurs millions of years before them, the big civilisations must have gone down into darkness. But perhaps somewhere— somewhere in some dying tropical rain forest, perhaps—there could have been a few tough, primitive people who could live on grubs, worms, snails, anything from green slime to fungus that would give them the food they needed to buy the time to adapt. The more Idris thought about it, the more he convinced himself that somehow terrestrial man—even if only a small tribe of savages—would find a way to endure. It was a crazy notion, of course. A fantasy. A wish fulfilment. But it was strong enough to enable him to endure or accept anything so long as there remained the chance that he would one day lift off for Earth.

Meanwhile, he determined to learn as much about Minerva as possible, to make himself acceptable to the Triple-T party if he could, and to appear to co-operate fully with Manfrius de Skun.

After he had slept, Zylonia took him back to the project centre for a medical check-up. Dr. de Skun seemed more than satisfied with the results.

Brain rhythms normal, pulse slightly fast, blood pressure normal, motor responses normal, temperature normal, eyesight normal. Almost a text-book example of a man in perfect health.

"Despite having terminated your recovery programme in such a dramatic fashion," said Dr. de Skun, "you are in remarkably good condition. There will be further check-ups, of course, but my work has ended. The technique of brain transplant into a cloned body has been triumphantly demonstrated." His face clouded. "On the physical level, at least. But there is still much work to be done before the process can be used for the benefit of all Minervans . . . You are a very intelligent man, Captain Hamilton." He smiled. "Perhaps a shade too intelligent for comfort. You have talked much—among other things—with Zylonia de Herrens . . . She is my daughter, by the way . . . Also you have read the *Creed*. So you will appreciate some of our difficulties. You see, although we have demonstrated physically that the technique is successful, we have yet to satisfy a large number of suspicious people—notably the Triple-T party—that it is psychologically successful. They need to be assured that you have an integrated personality."

"In other words," said Idris, "if I conform to Minervan standards and do not make any trouble, your immortality project will be accepted."

"Precisely." Manfrius de Skun sighed. "I could have wished that you were less intelligent, perhaps. It would have made matters easier . . . Actually, Captain Hamilton, I could have ensured that you were less intelligent. Over the years, we have made a very careful and detailed study of your brain. Certain areas—the areas associated with critical appraisal and decision-making, for example—could have been modified."

"I am grateful that you did not modify them."

110

"Ethically, I did not have the right. But it would have been so easy. So very easy."

"I am grateful to you, sir. And I admire your integrity."

Manfrius de Skun laughed grimly. "I may yet regret it. Already the Triple-T party regard you as a sort of cultural time-bomb."

Idris was silent for a moment or two. Then he said: "Dr. de Skun, I owe you much. No, that is a bloody understatement. I owe you all—my life, in fact. You really should have burned those nasty little areas of my brain when you had the chance. But I am conscious of my debt. I will do my best to behave as a model Minervan citizen for a time."

"How long is 'for a time'?"

"For as long as it takes you to get the necessary authority to proceed with your immortality process."

"And then?"

"And then," said Idris, throwing discretion aside, "I am going to find a crew for the *Amazonia* and blast off for Earth."

"You *are* mad."

"Don't worry too much, Dr. de Skun. It is a controlled madness."

"I could inform the Grand Council of your intentions."

"But you won't. It would only serve to show that I am not integrated. Therefore the end of the immortality process, and, on the present decline in Minervan life-span, the end of life on the tenth planet in the not-too-distant future . . . Incidentally, Zylonia has a surname different from yours. Why did you say she was your daughter?"

"We do not have marriage, Captain Hamilton. Therefore we use matrilinear descent. It is convenient."

"Stupid of me. I should have known." Idris grinned. "Maybe you did burn bits of my brain, after all."

21

THE LIFT CAME noiselessly to a halt. The doors opened.
Idris stepped out into the tower dome, which was illuminated by concealed strip lighting that ran in a slender ring
round its transparent walls. He peered through the vacuum
separated triple walls of plastiglass and could see nothing.
He was bitterly disappointed.

Zylonia was shivering and seemed afraid.

"Are you cold?"

"Psychologically cold. Few Minervans are at ease up
here. Down below is the world we have created—a world
of warmth and security. Up here, though we cannot feel it,
we are reminded of the deadness that lies outside."

"I can see nothing."

"You will." She touched a stud by the lift door, and the
dome darkened.

When his eyesight had adjusted Idris looked up and saw
the timeless unwinking brilliance of the stars. The sight
made him feel elated. It was a long time since he had seen
the stars. Fifty centuries. He tore his gaze from them
reluctantly, stepped close to the wall of the tower dome and
peered down. Presently, by starlight, he could make out a
few dim shapes—rocks, evidently. Some quite big, but
most of them small. He thought he could see the reflection
of stars in what looked like a pool of water. But, of course,
he had to be mistaken. Looking up again, he thought he

could see clouds obliterating some of the star patterns. But, again, he had to be mistaken. Probably some kind of fogging in the dome.

Idris gave a nervous laugh. "I'm having delusions. I think I can see clouds and water . . . I wish there were more light."

"Then, let there be light," said Zylonia. She touched another stud.

Suddenly, the terrain around the tower, for perhaps a radius of one kilometre, was brilliantly illuminated. Idris gazed out, fascinated, at a strange, stark wonderland. There were indeed clouds—large, fleecy, fluffy, like the clouds of Earth—drifting serenely through a black sky. There were indeed pools—one or two large enough to be called lakes, most small enough to be no more than puddles. And there were beautiful, crystalline rocks, glittering like massive diamonds.

Idris looked upwards, and was momentarily blinded by the light from what seemed to be an artificial sun.

"It's incredible," he said softly. "Quite incredible . . . The light — what is it?"

"An atomic lamp. It is on low intensity. It is set on a pylon three hundred metres high. At its present power, we can safely stay in the dome for about an hour. I can increase the level of illumination, but if I do our safety margin decreases proportionally. Would you like more light?"

"No, thank you. Not yet. Already there is so much to see . . . It's all so incredibly beautiful and amazing. I had anticipated a kind of lunar landscape—nothing but rocks and dust plains and mountains and craters. Instead, clouds, lakes. Astound me some more. Tell me that you also get snow and rain."

She gave a nervous laugh. "Yes, Idris, we do get snow and rain. Blizzards also. The atmosphere is helium. The clouds are hydrogen. They fall as hydrogen rain or hydrogen snow, depending upon slight variations in pressure and temperature."

"Then the lakes are hydrogen lakes?"

"Yes. The surface temperature is about seventeen degrees K. You are familiar with the Kelvin scale?"

He laughed. "Kelvin was a man of Earth . . . So the surface of Minerva is only seventeen degrees above absolute zero. And this frozen planet is the lost citadel of mankind. Something will have to be done about that."

"There is nothing to be done."

"Oh, yes, there is." He pointed. "What is that magnificent crystalline formation?"

Zylonia came to the plastiglass wall and followed his gaze. "Solid oxygen, probably. The nitrogen rocks are usually smaller and they do not reflect light quite so well. But, to be quite sure, we would have to consult a physicist."

Idris was entranced. "This is truly the Ice Queen's Palace."

"Please. I do not understand. What is the Ice Queen's Palace?"

"Part of an Earth legend, my dear. Created, I think, by a man called Hans Andersen . . . It was a story about a little boy who found the Ice Queen's Palace and was held in thrall by having a needle of ice plunged into his heart. But his childhood sweetheart followed him and melted the ice with her love. Then they were able to return to their own country."

Zylonia said: "I hope they lived happily ever after."

"Naturally. It was a convention of all such tales." Then he added irrelevantly: "There is no needle of ice in my heart. I shall return to my own country. I know it."

She took his hand. "Poor Idris. Who can blame you for harbouring impossible dreams? But, to please me, do not speak of them to other Minervans. It could be disturbing."

"Disturbing! That's a nice word." He laughed grimly. "Mankind now hibernates on the tenth planet and must not be disturbed."

"You know what I mean."

"Yes, I know what you mean. It is an axiom of *Talbot's Creed* that Earth is finished for ever. But I do not believe that. Perhaps I did once, but not now."

"Idris, you know the facts."

"Five thousand years is a long time. Facts can change. Five thousand years ago I was dead. Now I am alive. So much for facts."

Again she shivered. "I am cold. That dead world out there seems to project its coldness into my spirit. Let us go from this place. I promised to show you the surface of Minerva. You have seen it."

"Give me five more minutes, Zylonia. I know the surface is a place of terror to you, but to me it is beautiful. I can see why those early colonists wanted to build domed cities. It is a tragedy they didn't succeed. If they had, Minervan history would have been very different. Living on the surface, under the stars, you would all have been reminded that human destiny cannot be confined to a dead world. As it is you have all become afraid of open skies. You have developed the mole mentality."

"What is a mole?"

"A small, furry, half-blind creature of Earth. It lives underground and spends its time constructing elaborate tunnel systems in the quest for food." He gave a bitter laugh. "Who knows—perhaps Earth has now become a world fit for moles to live in."

Idris peered intently through the plastiglass. He could understand Zylonia's apprehension. The surface of Minerva was deadly; but it was also an exhilarating challenge. And, in a strange way, it was beautiful. In his mind's eye, he could see it filled with light and life. Domed cities, space ports—a civilisation dynamically expanding until it was ready to reclaim the entire solar system. But, after three thousand years, all the Minervans had achieved was a sub-terranean culture, zero population growth, and a pathological fear of changing the *status quo*.

"All right, Zylonia. I know you have had as much as you can take. So let us go back to the community of moles. But, one day, I am going to drive you all out into the open —before that bloody creed has entirely brainwashed the sense of adventure out of the mind of man."

22

THE RHYTHM OF the M-day was maintained in the subterranean cities of Minerva simply by a dim-out of the lighting in streets and avenues and other public places in the Five Citics. Most Minervans observed the conventions of night and day for obvious and practical reasons. But, apart from the necessity of shift-work or the watch system for the atomic generators, the re-cycling plant, the hydroponics installations, the vast air-conditioning system and other life-support units that had to be operated continuously, there were some Minervans who preferred to reverse natural conditioning and live by night. They were mostly poets, artists, social discontents—as Idris discovered. On Earth, at one time, they would have been defined as drop-outs.

The Five Cities were called Talbot, Vorshinski, Brandt, Aragon, and Chiang, after the original leaders of the colonists. The cities formed a rough subterranean pentagon, each city being approximately five kilometres from its neighbours. Inter-city transit was by means of monorail cars. It was the custom of many of the discontents to ride the cars throughout the night, holding informal discussions, parties, protest meetings until the early hours. Eventually, Idris established contact with a group of young dreamers who were dissatisfied with the Minervan way of life. Eventually he took a desperate course of action that was to split Minervan society and destroy the centuries-old authoritarianism.

116

But, before that happened, he spent a great deal of time familiarising himself with all that had been accomplished on Minerva. Also he endured an exhausting programme of interviews and discussions with historians, sociologists, psychologists, anthropologists and others interested in the decline and fall of the civilisations of Earth. He bore their questions patiently and answered them to the best of his ability. As a piece of walking, talking history, he tried to be objective and honest in his analysis of the collapse of terrestrial man. Above all, he tried not to be provocative. For the time being, it was his intention to be accepted as normal, if possible, by Minervan standards.

For a while, Zylonia was his constant companion. It was she who took him on his first tour of the Five Cities. During the course of his tour he met many Minervans, all of whom had seen him already on tri-di. In fact, not only had they already seen him as he now was, they had also seen a documentary presentation of the entire immortality project, beginning with shots of the salvage operation on the *Dag Hammarskjold* (Idris learned that the wreckage of the *Dag* had been placed in a permanent orbit round Minerva so that it might eventually be brought down as a valuable museum piece) and proceeding to shots of the immensely difficult low-temperature surgery needed to remove the brain of the dead captain for resuscitation procedure. Different stages of the cloning technique had been shown, as had sequences in the simulated cabin, when Idris had been no more than a brain in a tank, able to use a synthetic eye, and when Zylonia was acting as the reality-anchor meant to preserve his sanity.

The immortality project, which might never have developed if Minervan radio telescopes had not tracked the stricken space-ship, was currently the issue that dominated Minervan conversation, philosophy and politics. For the first time in the history of mankind, it had been demonstrated that the failure of the entire organic life-support system—the body—need not result in the permanent death of the personality, now incontrovertibly shown to be seated in the brain. Provide that brain with an identical life-support

117

system—and the psychosomatic potential and responses of a cloned body would be the same as the original—and the continuation of personality could be assured until the neural circuits of the brain became so supersaturated with data in the form of memories, desires and conditioned responses that it could no longer function as a rational entity. In other words, physical senility had been conquered. Because of the cloning technique which had worked so successfully for a body and its brain which had been dead for five thousand years, Minervans could now look forward to centuries of creative existence. All that there remained to conquer was mental senility—the ultimate breakdown of overloaded neural systems. The last enemy.

Dr. Manfrius de Skun, the psycho-surgeon responsible for the breakthrough, the man who had devoted so much of his life to bringing Idris Hamilton back from the dead, had suddenly become one of the most important, influential and controversial men on Minerva. The Triple-T party closed its ranks and tended to regard him as a kind of latter-day Satan come to tempt the pure with the promise of extended life. The more liberal-minded Minervans regarded him simply as a saviour—the man who had discovered how to delay the approach of everlasting night.

But the outcome of the struggle depended entirely on whether Dr. de Skun's guinea pig--Captain Idris Hamilton —could be shown to be a completely sane individual. There were many who hoped that slight deviations from accepted standards of normal behaviour—normal Minervan behaviour —could be shown to be symptoms of an underlying instability.

As he talked to the various Minervans that he met, Idris soon learned to distinguish those who were in favour of the immortality project from those who were against it, though all of them seemed to be invariably and almost monotonously polite. The difference lay in their questions. Those in favour of the project—mostly younger people, scientists, technicians and the like—asked him chiefly about his memories of life on Earth. Those who were against the project—administrators, some teachers and a number of older women of various skills—questioned him most on his reactions to Minervan society. Idris recognized most of the loaded questions and did his best to be diplomatic. On the whole, Zylonia was pleased with his performance.

She took him to Vorshinski Farm. Each of the Five Cities had its own organic farm, which was quite separate from the hydroponics plants and the protein factories. Synthetic steak, chicken breast, fish and cheese were standard components of Minervan diet. But organic food was also produced—largely for children, hospital patients and the very old.

Vorshinski Farm held a special place in Zylonia's affection. She had taken her therapeutic work-holiday there. But there was also another reason—as Idris discovered to his ultimate disadvantage.

The farm was impressive. It was a vast natural cave that had been discovered by seismic survey centuries ago. It was nearly five hundred metres below Vorshinski City; and the only approach to it was by lift, down a broad service shaft.

It did not look at all like a cave. It was, as Idris had to admit, a magnificent illusion. Looking up, he did not see rock-face dripping with condensation. He saw what seemed to be a blue sky—as blue as it had been once on Earth before pollution brought the long twilight and the everlasting rain—a blue sky flecked with fleecy cloud, and a bright sun high overhead. At Vorshinski Farm it was high summer, with the cornfields turning a smoky golden colour. With cattle—Friesians, Red Poll, Herefordshires and even a few Texas Long Horns, browsing on succulent grass. With pigs running in the orchards to gobble up windfalls. With free range hens scratching for grubs and insects where the pigs had torn up the grass and exposed the top soil. With butterflies on the wing, even, and with bees tirelessly searching for nectar.

Idris was astounded. Here, far below the surface of a dead planet, was an almost perfect facsimile of a rural environment in the Golden Age of Earth. He looked in vain for

119

the plants and animals that had been genetically adapted to flourish under the harsh conditions of Mars, and was surprised when he could not find any. Then, after a moment or two, he understood the reason. Why bother with low-yield crops and livestock bred chiefly for their survival qualities in a poor environment when you can create an ideal environment for high-yield farm systems?

The controlled climate, as he learned from the farm manager, was designed on the theoretical optimum that might have been achieved for the best agricultural areas in the temperate zones of Earth at the peak of organic food production in the twentieth century, before men had really begun to poison the soil, air and water which supported life.

The mobile atomic lamp that was Vorshinski's artificial sun delivered a variable, computer-controlled level of radiant energy, determined by the growth rate of the crops and the condition of the stock. Periodic showers were also computer controlled. The artificial rain that fell was channelled into two small streams feeding a central lake where ducks dabbled and freshwater fish swam, and from which the water was pumped once more to the rain reservoir. Although the cereals, vegetables and root crops grown on the farm were Earth varieties, they were, as Sirius Bourne, the farm manager, explained to Idris, accelerated strains. Most of them matured in less than half the time it used to take for similar crops to mature on Earth. It was the same with the live stock. At Vorshinski Farm, the four-season cycle had been transformed into a three-season cycle: a short spring, a long summer, and a very short autumn/winter period. The three-season cycle could be operated twice in little more than one E-year.

Sirius Bourne was a pleasant young man. By Earth reckoning, he looked to be about thirty years old. He and Zylonia obviously had much affection for each other—a fact which disconcerted Idris and had disastrous results.

However, all went reasonably well until the time came to leave. Sirius held Zylonia's hands and kissed her on both cheeks.

Then he said: "When shall we put our slippers under the same bed again, Zylonia? It has been a long time. I was very happy with you."

"Soon," said Zylonia calmly. "I have been working very hard with Idris, as you know. But soon, definitely. I would like that."

Idris stared at them in dismay. "You were lovers?"

Sirius laughed. "Forgive me. That is a romantic Earth concept. But, as you say, we were lovers. While you were still in the tank and your clone body was being cultured, Zylonia and I entered a short-term pairing. It was good for her, good for me. She is a delicious person to have sex with, don't you think? Her body is so responsive. I can remember the time when we drank a little too much before, and —"

Idris hit him. Unthinkingly, he lashed out and with one blow destroyed all the goodwill he had been building up. There were witnesses—two farm technicians.

Sirius lay on the grass under an apple tree, staring up at Idris in amazement. Blood trickled from his mouth. He tried to wipe it away and only succeeded in smearing his face.

"Please, I do not understand. Why did you do that?"

Idris was beyond reason. "Stand up," he said icily.

Sirius picked himself up, and Idris hit him again.

Once more he fell to the grass. There was blood over his eye this time. Idris had flipped, and knew that he had flipped. But he didn't care. He was enjoying it.

Zylonia screamed. The technicians tried to intervene. They regretted it. Idris kicked one in the stomach and hit the other one's arm with a flat-hand blow that would have smashed a brick.

Again Zylonia screamed. This time the sound of her voice seemed to penetrate the black anger in his head.

"Beast!" she shouted. "Beast! Madman! Talbot was right. Earth people take the lust for destruction with them wherever they go. Why did we waste so much effort to bring you back to life? You are nothing but a destroyer, Idris. Nothing but a beast of the jungle."

Then she sank to her knees, weeping, as she realised what she had said. She had declared Idris to be mad, in front of witnesses. She, who had worked so hard for the immortality project, had now ruined it.

Idris gazed at her, helplessly. Then he looked at the three men he had injured. Sirius Bourne had a smashed face, one eye totally closed. The technician who had been kicked in the guts was still writhing and gasping; but, from the strength of the kick, Idris knew that he was not severely damaged. The other technician moaned and held his forearm. It hung strangely. With a sick feeling inside him, Idris knew that he had broken it.

23

BECAUSE THERE WAS so little crime in the Five Cities, Minerva did not need the numerous law-enforcement officers, judges, advocates and the personnel who had been a feature of the civilisations that had existed on Earth and Mars. Without a monetary system, there was little temptation to steal. Personal possessions were few and utilitarian. If they were lost, broken or worn out, new ones could be obtained on demand at the Commissariat. Violence was minimal, since all Minervans were conditioned to abhor it from infancy. But perhaps the greatest deterrent was that, in the Five Cities, there was no place where a criminal could hope to hide and remain undetected for any length of time. It would, of course, be possible to escape to the surface by any of the five towers and their air-locks. But that would require a continuous life-support system, which could not be obtained.

Two or three times in the course of an M-year, there were cases of assault or rape—usually associated with over-indulgence in alcohol on the part of the culprit, and usually treated as psychological illness. The last murder had been committed seven M-years before Idris attacked Sirius Bourne and his colleagues at Vorshinski Farm. The murderer had anticipated the course of justice by exiling himself to the sur-face and, space-suited, walking into the nearest hydrogen lake, where he 'pulled the plug' and died instantly.

The case of Idris Hamilton was, therefore, a sensation. The crime of assault causing grievous bodily harm had been committed on Vorshinski territory and would normally have been dealt with by officers of the city council—the president acting as judge, the councillors acting as jury, and the city warden as prosecutor; the accused being allowed to conduct his own defence or to nominate any person of his choice. It was mandatory that whoever was chosen by the accused to represent him must accept the charge, irrespective of his own wishes. If the accused felt that a local trial might prejudice his interests, he had the right to demand Trial by Five. In which case the judge would still be the president of Vorshinski Council, but the jury would consist of the presidents of the other four city councils.

Idris chose Trial by Five and appointed Dr. Manfrius de Skun for his defence.

The issue to be decided was not simply whether he had attacked Sirius Bourne and injured the farm manager's colleagues. Idris was prepared to plead guilty with a defence of unreasonable provocation. But he realised that the true aim of the trial would be to determine whether or not he was sane according to the Minervan concept of sanity. If it could be established by tricky argument that he was not wholly sane, he knew that Dr. de Skun's immortality project would be destroyed. In a sense, two men were on trial. By appointing Manfrius de Skun as his defence advocate, Idris was not only employing the man who knew more about him than anyone else on Minerva, he was also giving Dr. de Skun a chance to present his own case.

It was not a long trial. And it was soon evident to Idris that the verdict had been reached before the trial started. He learned later that three of the presidents were Triple-T men. This was their opportunity to make speeches about long-established values and the importance of preserving the *status quo*.

Dr. de Skun fought brilliantly. Regardless of the fact that his own daughter was the chief witness for the prosecution, he subjected her to merciless interrogation, showing that, in the course of her professional duties, she had become personally involved with the accused and had encouraged him in the belief that she had genuine affection for him. To Zylonia's obvious discomfort, he made her describe the physical aspect of her relationship with Idris, thus seeking to establish that what might be regarded as violence by Minervan standards was accepted behaviour by Earth standards. He then went on to show that Idris Hamilton was the product of a culture where sexual possession was the accepted norm. Thus, for such a person, it would be normal behaviour by his own standards to react violently when the woman who had become his love-object was again desired by someone who had previously possessed her in the sexual connotations normal to the Earth culture of five thousand years ago.

Dr. de Skun was a brilliant defence advocate. Logically, he had established that Idris Hamilton's actions at Vorshinski Farm, though extravagant, were not outside the parameters of behaviour that might be expected from a typical Earth man.

But to no avail.

The verdict was guilty as charged, by reason of mental instability. In his summing up, the president of Vorshinski Council allowed himself to publicly castigate Dr. de Skun. He expressed the view that severe restrictions should be placed on aspects of research and experimentation involving the human brain. He had, he said drily, the greatest respect for Dr. de Skun as a scientist and for his motive in desiring to extend human life. But perhaps his enthusiasm had blinded him to certain psychological and moral dangers involved in transplanting the human brain. Men were not mere animals, they were creatures of finely balanced reason and emotion. The case before the court tended to indicate that, despite the technical brilliance and physical success of the resuscitation and subsequent brain transplant of the Earth man, Idris Hamilton, the danger of resulting mental abnormality was serious enough to cast grave doubts upon the value of such techniques.

And so on. The president of Vorshinski Council, Arman Bilas, was a pompous man. He went on at great length about the role of science in society. Science, he said, making a feeble joke which was noisily appreciated by his colleagues, was much too serious a matter to be left to the scientists. He hoped that, in view of this particular case—which, mercifully was not as serious as it might have been—the Five Cities Council might opportunely question the value of current research projects. It may well be that some scientists could find more useful employment in other fields.

Dr. de Skun bravely sat through the assassination of his immortality project, his face blank, expressionless. Idris felt immensely sorry for him and immensely ashamed. A lifetime's work had been destroyed because one stupid Earth man had failed to control his emotional reactions. Manfrius de Skun had given him a new life—and this was his reward.

Finally the president came to the sentence.

"Idris Hamilton, you have been found guilty of the crime of violent and unprovoked aggression, causing injury to persons who did not in any way attempt to injure you. Were you a Minervan, without any previous history of mental abnormality, this court would prescribe a rigorous course of treatment. However, there are extenuating circumstances —unique circumstances, I may say. You are an Earth man, a resuscitated Earth man, whose brain has been transferred from its dead body to a life-support system, and from the life-support system to a new body. It is the opinion of this court that such procedures can cause great psychological distress, and that therefore you cannot be held to be wholly responsible for your actions. Therefore, I sentence you to ninety days' confinement, during which time you will receive psychiatric treatment, and at the end of which time you will be examined by a panel consisting of myself and two qualified advisers. We shall then determine if you are in a condition which justifies our releasing you, so that you may resume your place in society. Have you anything to say?"

Idris had a great deal to say. But he glanced at Manfrius de Skun. Dr. de Skun shook his head. With considerable reluctance, Idris remained silent.

"It is our judgement also," went on the president, "that though you will be allowed visitors during your confinement, under no circumstances can you be allowed to see Zylonia de Herrens. This court is now adjourned."

24

THE IMPRISONMENT WAS not rigorous. By Earth standards it was positively luxurious. Idris was the only occupant in a group of three cells that were really part of Vorshinski Hospital. His room was comfortable and well-furnished. He had tri-di and book tapes. Every day he was taken under escort to a gymnasium for exercise. Every day a psychiatrist visited him. Sometimes, he was allowed a solitary swim in the hospital pool. He liked the swimming sessions enormously. Apart from the sheer pleasure of splashing about freely in water, the feeling of apparent weightlessness reminded him of the time he had spent in space.

The psychiatrist was a mild-mannered old man who seemed far more interested in Idris's recollections of Earth and in playing chess than in any overt analysis. But perhaps that was part of the treatment, thought Idris. Lull the patient into feeling secure, then start the heavy stuff when he least expects it. He didn't mind. The psychiatrist didn't look the kind who would do his patient a great deal of harm. In fact during the whole of his imprisonment there never was any 'heavy stuff'—no drugs, no probing of childhood passions, no seeking of repressed desires. His brain rhythms were monitored regularly, along with heart, blood pressure, weight and general physical condition. The psychiatric treatment—if, indeed there ever was any psychiatric treatment—was painless and unnoticeable.

For a while, Idris thought a great deal about Zylonia. For a while, he desperately wanted to see her, talk to her, make love to her. But as time passed, the desire lessened. Perhaps, he told himself grimly, the Minervans were loading his diet with sedatives. It didn't seem to matter.

Manfrius de Skun came to see him early in his confinement. He brushed aside Idris's apologies impatiently.

"My dear friend—I hope I may call you my friend—you must not think so badly of yourself. It is we Minervans who are at fault. We should have educated you more fully in Minervan customs and attitudes—that was my responsibility. And we should have made more allowance for your violent behaviour." He shrugged. "But, as you know, the matter became political rather than scientific, and so we have both suffered. I am sorry."

"Your kindness is unnerving. You spend years of your life bringing me back from the dead, whereupon I make love to your daughter, involve you and her in a public scandal, and succeed in destroying your life's work. I would not blame you if you wanted to tear my brain out of its new head and toss it back into the void." Idris gave a bitter laugh. "There are some things that do not change. On the Earth I knew, as here on Minerva, men of your stature were frequently thrown to the wolves."

"Please, what is wolves?"

"A wolf is—was—a ferocious quadruped that hunted in packs."

Dr. de Skun smiled. "Ah, yes. I perceive the metaphor. Do not be distressed, Idris. My immortality project will rise again. Science is never permanently defeated."

Idris was silent for a moment or two. Then he said: "You are an honest man, Dr. de Skun. The least I can do is to be honest with you. I hope your immortality project is never brought back."

Manfrius de Skun raised an eyebrow. "Why? It has benefited you. Why can it not benefit thousands of Minervans? You are aware, surely, that our life expectation is decreasing?"

"It may be a good thing for any individual, but it is not a good thing for mankind. You see, it offers absolute security. Mankind must expand or perish. It is an ancient law. Minervan society is already static, inward-looking not outward-looking. The promise of extended life will reduce what is left of mankind to the level of living fossils, whose only purpose is to prolong individual existence . . . Perhaps I am just a simple barbarian, Dr. de Skun, or perhaps I am psychotic; but I believe that man must continually try to extend his dominion or perish. Minerva is the last outpost of the race that once flourished on the third planet. If your people do not attempt to re-colonise the solar system, billions of years of evolution will have been in vain. And they will not make such an effort unless they are threatened with extinction. Do you follow me?"

"Yes, I follow your reasoning, Idris. It hurts, but it has the ring of truth." Dr. de Skun's face registered pain. Then suddenly he smiled. "But, in any case, my work has been of value, Idris, because it has produced you. You are the catalyst. You are the only person who can change our overall thinking. It is a heavy responsibility . . . How are you getting along with your psychiatrist?"

Idris said: "Do you think this room is bugged?"

"Bugged? I do not understand."

"Do you think there are any listening or recording devices? I have had a good look round, and I can't find any. But I am not an expert."

Dr. de Skun looked shocked. "Of course it is not bugged, as you call it. Everyone—even a person in detention—is entitled to privacy. It would be unethical not to allow you to talk to your friends in complete freedom."

"It will take me some time to understand Minervan ethics," retorted Idris drily. "My simulated cabin was bugged, you may recall."

"You were not bugged, as you call it," said Dr. de Skun, making a fine distinction. "It was a monitoring system, vital to your treatment."

Idris laughed. "The same philosophy may apply now."

"I assure you it does not. You are now being treated as an ordinary Minervan would be treated, if he had committed an act of transgression."

"Dr. de Skun, I am afraid you place too much faith in the Queensberry Rules. And, to anticipate your question, that is another metaphor. The Queensberry Rules were drawn up to establish fair play in boxing, a sport in which two Earth men tried to batter each other into insensibility by striking with their fists. But, since I have found no bugging devices, I will go along with your belief . . . To answer your question, I get along fine with my psychiatrist. I feed him fairy tales to keep him happy; we play chess—he lacks the killer instinct, I may say—and I tell him what it was like on Earth before darkness began to fall from the air . . . How is Zylonia? By Minervan standards, I seem to have treated her very badly."

"She is well," said Manfrius de Skun evenly. "She sends her greetings, and hopes that you are well also. She has time-paired with Sirius Bourne. I think they are happy together for the time being."

Idris gave a deep sigh. "That figures. When you see her, tell her that I wish her all the luck in the world—this world. Tell her that I am sorry I tried to smash Sirius . . . No, don't tell her that. It would only destroy her faith in barbarians."

Manfrius de Skun shrugged. "You are a strange man, Idris. But I respect you, and I believe that you have much to give us Minervans."

"You are essentially a good man, Dr. de Skun; and I respect you also. But, like many great scientists, you are naive. Do not expect too much of me. Then you will not be disappointed."

"I will come again," said Manfrius de Skun. "We will have further conversation. It is instructive—mutually so, I hope."

"It is indeed. I shall look forward to your next visit."

But Dr. de Skun did not come again. A few days later he died of heart failure. Apart from the revolutionary brain transplant technique, the Minervans had long ago perfected the processes of heart transplant. But, in view of the political situation, the Triple-T party held the power of veto. A suitable heart was available, its former owner having committed suicide by leaping on a monorail at the right time. But the Triple-T people ensured that the heart was used to restore life to a compatible woman capable of bearing children.

As part of his immortality project, Dr. de Skun had arranged for a cloned body to be cultured. It was ready to receive his brain. But, once more, the Triple-T party exercised the power of veto. Both the body of Dr. de Skun and the cloned body were fed into the Minervan re-cycling system.

Idris did not learn of this for some time. He regarded it as murder by default.

25

DURING THE COURSE of his ninety-day term, Idris received two more visitors. Both were women.

The first was Mary Evans, the teacher, the woman of Earth, whose hair was white, though she was still physically young, and upon whose face sadness had inscribed many fine lines.

"Well, Captain Hamilton, and how are you?"

"Well, Miss Evans. And how are you?"

"I have come to offer myself," she said bluntly. "You must have need of a woman . . . I am told — I understand — that Zylonia de Herrens has other commitments. So I thought . . ." She faltered.

"Who sent you?"

"No one sent me. I just came. Do you want me to go away?"

"No. Stay—please. I am suspicious. Surely, it is understandable. Why did you really come?"

"I have told you. I came to offer myself." She began to cry. "Stupid, isn't it? Why should you want a woman with white hair and sagging breasts? When you get out of here, you can probably time-pair with every third woman on Minerva. You are a celebrity. But I thought . . . I thought . . ." She held her head in her hands and sobbed convulsively.

Idris stroked her hair. Thirty-four years old, he thought.

White hair and sagging breasts. Unfulfilled. But I will make her hair glisten and her breasts proud. Because she is the last woman of Earth and I am the last man. Such a bond is stronger than sex. Such a bond is *vital*.

He held her close.

"You don't love me," sobbed Mary. "How can you love me? I am prematurely old. We don't even know each other. We are complete strangers."

"My darling Earth woman," he said. "Forget about Zylonia. Help *me* to forget about Zylonia. But you and I are of Earth's blood. For that alone we must love each other. Your white hair is a battle honour. Your breasts are Earth breasts and, therefore, beautiful . . . Now let us pull ourselves together and talk."

"If you want me to stay," she said, "I can do. I have permission from the President of Vorshinski."

Again he was suspicious. "Did you ask him, or did he ask you?"

"I asked him. Was it wrong of me? I'm sorry if I did the wrong thing . . . I won't stay unless you really want me to."

Idris was silent for a moment or two. Then he said: "These people are being very accommodating. I wonder why? First, they give me ninety days in a de luxe cooler. Then they agree to let me have the consolations of sex. I wonder why?"

Mary gave him a sad smile. "I imagine I am supposed to be a safety valve. They regard you as a kind of half-wild animal, Idris. I think they would like you to release your inhibitions with someone of your own kind, rather than corrupt the fair women of Minerva."

"Yes, I am a savage," he said with grim satisfaction. "Unlike your perfectly adjusted Minervans who are never violent and who are content merely to survive in their technological ant-hill, I have delusions of grandeur. I am dangerous. I react violently when provoked. And I am determined that what is left of the human race shall *live* again. If it involves corrupting the fair women of Minerva—a delicious phrase—and breaking the arms of their socially adjusted males, I'll do it. The only way they can stop me is to kill me. I understand they have no death penalty. So that's one thing going for me . . . If you decide to stay with me, how do you know that I won't beat you, or even kill you?"

She gave a deep sigh. "I have lived with the Minervans longer than you have, Idris. In some ways, I admire them. In other ways, they terrify me. They have virtually eliminated the aggressive instinct—which may or may not be a good thing—but they are so devastatingly hygienic, both physically and psychologically." She laughed. "Perhaps it would be a good thing to be beaten by an Earth man, even to be killed by an Earth man. I'll take my chance."

"I like you, Mary Evans."

"I like you, Idris Hamilton."

"Well, then, we must plan for the future. By my reckoning, I have forty-seven M-days left to serve. You will share them with me?"

"Yes."

"I cannot guarantee that I will be good to you in the accepted sense—in the sense that such a statement is understood by Earth people. I cannot guarantee that, when my sentence is over, I will be docile according to Minervan standards. In fact, I can guarantee nothing. If you form an affection for me, or I for you, there could be much heartache."

"I'll take my chance. You are the last Earth man. Perhaps, even, the last man. I'll take my chance."

He kissed her, held her close. Strangely, the sagging breasts did not seem to sag any more. They were firm against him. Firm and responsive.

"There is something else I have to tell you," said Mary. "Manfrius de Skun is dead. He had a heart attack. He could have been saved. As you must know, transplant surgery has been developed to a very high level here. But the Triple-T people were strong enough to veto resuscitation, transplant and even the use of his cloned body . . . That is the way these people deal with rebels, Idris. They do not execute them. They contain them and wait patiently. Then they let nature take its course."

He was silent for a while. At length, he said: "Manfrius de Skun was a good man, quite possibly a great one. History will decide. He spent his best years bringing me back to life and giving me a new body . . . I am Manfrius de Skun's Joker, Mary. He slipped me into the pack. Now take off your clothes and come to bed. I warn you, I am going to do my damnedest to get you with child."

26

THE PSYCHIATRIST DID not approve of the presence of Mary Evans. She was a distraction. She seemed—unintentionally, no doubt—to weaken the trust relationship he hoped to establish with Idris. Nevertheless, he knew there were subtle political reasons why the Earth man should be allowed to have the company of this particular woman during his treatment. He kept his nose out of politics; but he was aware of vague plans in certain quarters to discredit Idris Hamilton yet further.

Mary did her best to fit into the necessary routine. When the psychiatrist made his visit, she was allowed out to stroll in the avenues of Vorshinski City. But she took all her meals with Idris, exercised with him, watched tri-di with him, talked with him, slept with him.

There was much impersonal passion in their love-making. It was, as Idris saw it, not so much a joining of Idris Hamilton and Mary Evans as a joining of the last Earth man and the last true Earth woman. You could not count the children, he reasoned, though they were born of Earth. Their conditioning and their attitudes must now be almost wholly Minervan. Earth bodies, but Minervan minds . . . .

So the union with Mary was a symbolic union. Sometimes, fantasising, he saw himself as a middle-aged Adam and Mary as a slightly bedraggled Eve. Sometimes, fantasising, he imagined the two of them returning to Earth, the

Garden of Eden that was less than a hundred million miles from the sun, and repopulating it. In more rational moments, he could laugh at his dreams. Between them, the new Adam and Eve would produce a disastrously limited genetic fool.

Minervan drama, as seen on the tri-di, was pathetically naive and amateurish. It contained no violence—either physical or mental. It was pure domestic drama, full of Utopian ideals, manufactured by zombies for zombies. Most of it consisted of variations on a theme: A wished to time-pair with B; B wished to time-pair with C; C was wholly absorbed in the development of a new hydroponics/socio-logical/electronic/medical/atomic project and had a faithful assistant who desperately wanted to bear C's child or become pregnant by C, depending upon the sex of A, B and C. The denouement was usually democratic, eminently mature, providing satisfaction for all parties—and as boring as hell.

Where was drama that could equal *Oedipus Rex, Julius Caesar, The Masterbuilder, St. Joan, Cat on a Hot Tin Roof?* Lost in the mists of time. There were, apparently, no Minervan dramatists with the brilliance of Shakespeare, the passion of an Ibsen, the earthiness of a Tennessee Williams. There were just no Minervan dramatists. They were all too goddamned safe. They never suffered, they were never threatened, they were never called upon to make sacrifices. They were the perfect hygienic products of a perfect hygienic welfare state. They were zombies.

It was the same with music. Nothing to compare, however remotely, with Bach, Beethoven, Brahms—even Strauss. No fire. No passion. No violence. The best that could be offered was comparable to the worst of Mozart. Even the folk music and songs had a uniform dullness.

The Minervans had obviously a brilliant command of science and technology to enable them to maintain a stable population on or under a frozen planet for thirty centuries but, somehow, the artistic impulse—the creative imagination that gives meaning to life—seemed to have died. And all that was left of mankind now were ten thousand hygienic, totally adjusted zombies, a handful of brainwashed Earth children, a resuscitated middle-aged Adam and a faded Eve. The odds were pretty heavy against getting a replay of the Garden of Eden set-up.

Or so Idris thought until his second female visitor appeared.

She had the entirely delightful name of Damaris de Gaulle. The surname was familiar. Idris racked his brains. Some time in the twentieth century, he recalled, there had been a French general called de Gaulle, who had played a minor part in the Second World War. Perhaps this girl had some distant, tenuous kinship with him.

Damaris de Gaulle was very young. She could hardly be much more than ten M-years old, less than twenty E-years. She had long, blonde, flowing hair, slightly coarse features, and a well-formed body that would be good for child-bearing.

She gave a cool, self-assured and rather hostile glance at Mary, and confined her conversation to Idris.

"We know that this room is not monitored in any way, so it is possible to talk freely," she said. "I will be honest and direct with you. I would like you to be honest and direct with me."

"Who are we?" asked Idris.

"It is not important. But we call ourselves the Friends of the Ways. We are young people. We are night people. May I call you Captain?"

Idris laughed. "You may call me what you wish. Captain, if you like. It is singularly inappropriate because I lost my last command. But that does not matter. Why have you come to see me? Curiosity? The barbaric Earth man at bay?"

Damaris smiled. "They call you the Jesus Freak, but I prefer Captain. It is more dignified. It has a ring of authority."

"Who calls me the Jesus Freak?"

"The Friends of the Ways. It is because of an ancient myth. You must know it, of course. There was once a man of Earth called Jesus—one of the Friends who is a historian

139

claims that his real name was Joshua bar David, but no matter—who was executed for revolutionary activity. But somebody called Judas Pilate resuscitated him by a brain transplant, and he then founded the first true commune in Soviet Russia. It flourished mightily, I understand, until the capitalist countries of the west bombed it to extinction . . . The Friends of the Ways call you the Jesus Freak because of obvious parallels and because they hope you will lead them to establish a new commune that is free from the dreadful constrictions of *Talbot's Creed*. Will you lead them?"

With a considerable effort, Idris restrained the impulse to laugh. It was understandable that the Minervans had telescoped Earth's history. But, Jesus Lenin strikes again! That was hard to swallow.

"Who are you asking me to lead?"

"The youth of Minerva."

"All the youth of Minerva?"

Damaris tossed back her golden hair. "All the youth of Minerva who want to destroy this fossilized system of existence," she said. "When you are released, Captain, travel the ways at night. You will find us. And if you are truly the Jesus Freak, you will help us. You will lead us to the creation of a Great Society. Now I must go . . . Will you lead us?"

"I will meet your Friends of the Ways. If they are worth leading, I will lead them to something. I cannot promise that it will be a Soviet commune. I can promise that it will be better than *Talbot's Creed* and the static society you have now."

"That is good enough for us," said Damaris de Gaulle.

When she had gone, Mary said: "You are hellbent on destroying yourself, Idris."

"No, love," he retorted tranquilly. "I am hellbent on saving myself. Somehow, I and you are going back to Earth. You have a child in your belly, though you have not yet told me. He will walk on the soil of his home planet or I will die getting him there. Do you read me?"

"I read you," said Mary Evans, her eyes suddenly bright. "I read you loud and clear."

27

WHEN IDRIS WAS released after serving his term of 'corrective treatment', his freedom was made conditional. He was already resigned to the indefinite ban on any contact, other than chance meeting in a public place, with Zylonia de Herrens. But his release order contained other and more sinister restrictions.

He was released into the custody of Mary Evans, who was required to stand surety for his good behaviour. This meant simply that when he next transgressed—*if* he transgressed—Mary might suffer also. Two for the price of one. It was, he realised instantly, a kind of blackmail. Though no orthodox Minervan would have regarded it as such.

More sinister was the fact that he was required to report to the psychiatric clinic of Vorshinski Hospital every ten days for E.E.G. brain rhythm analysis and for subjective interrogation by a psychiatrist empowered to use a sophisticated kind of polygraph to determine whether or not his answers were truthful.

He was also required not to attend or address any public meeting or gathering—carefully defined as a group of not less than five people—without prior notice to and approval by the President of Vorshinski Council.

Most sinister of all, he was required until further notice (which probably meant for ever) to abstain from contributing to the genetic pool. Which meant, simply, that he was not allowed to fertilize any female.

But Mary was already pregnant. As soon as the fact were discovered—and it could not be hidden for very long—she would have to undergo compulsory abortion; and quite probably both she and Idris would be punished. Even apart from the ban on Idris, every pregnancy had to have prior approval, a fact of which Mary had been aware, though she had shut it out of her mind, probably because she desperately wanted to be pregnant by Idris. The Adam and Eve syndrome . . .

The fact that perfect birth-control was freely available would make the pregnancy look like a deliberate flouting of Minervan law.

One way or another, Idris realised, the Triple-T faction was going to be able to completely discredit the last Earth man. Time was on their side. Then any hope he might have entertained of peacefully persuading the Minervans to abandon their policy of psychological hibernation would be utterly ruined.

If anything was to be done about the situation, it would have to be done quickly.

Mary Evans had an apartment in Talbot City, uncomfortably near the home—if you could call a standardised living module a home—of Zylonia de Herrens. Idris had been offered a module of his own, ironically the apartment of the late Manfrius de Skun in central Vorshinski. It had been stripped of any possessions left by its previous occupant, and it looked pretty much the same as the other living units he had seen. But he would not take it. Though he did not believe in ghosts, he had too much respect and affection for the man who had brought him back from the dead to take over what had been his home and impose a new personality on it.

So he moved into Mary's apartment. And, on the first night of freedom, because he had little to lose, he left Mary at home in bed, blissfully exhausted after a passionate love-making, and went to seek the Friends of the Ways.

The automated transport that connected the Five Cities was not unlike the underground railways that had once existed in such cities as London, Paris and Moscow. Except

142

that the monorail cars were open to the crystalline and pleasantly illuminated surfaces of the tunnels; and there were no guards, drivers, ticket collectors. The movement of cars from station to station was smooth, fast, almost silent, unattended and free. The monorail service operated automatically round the clock. In the arbitrary morning of the M-day, it carried manual labourers, skilled workers, technicians, bureaucrats, scientists to their posts. In the small hours, it still carried a number of shift-workers and late visitors but it also carried the Friends of the Ways. The Night People. The rebellious youth of Minerva who had made the public cars of the monorail system their own meeting place.

Idris boarded a car at Talbot. It was empty. The car stayed at Talbot station for a few moments. Then a taped voice said quietly: "Please do not board or leave this car. Please do not board or leave this car." Then a buzzer sounded, and the car sped evenly along the tunnel to Vorshinski. The journey was not long. The Five Cities were separated from each other by only a few kilometres. Between one city and the next, there were two or three small request stops where the cars did not stop, though they slowed down considerably, unless a passenger pressed one of the red buttons that were placed near every seat.

The taped voice announced each sub-station in advance. "You are now approaching Talbot Farm . . . You are now approaching Talbot Hydroponics . . . You are now approaching Vorshinski Power . . ."

Because the cars were open, with only a transparent plastic screen at the front, there was the illusion of a warm, pleasant wind in the tunnel. Idris liked the invigorating feel of the artificial wind in his hair. It reminded him of the winds of Earth.

At Vorshinski Power, as the car slowed on its run through the sub-station, two figures came to the edge of the platform and vaulted neatly and expertly over the low sides of the car. They could have halted the car had they so wished. Each sub-station was equipped with request-stop buttons. But, evidently, they preferred this athletic and somewhat dangerous way of boarding a car.

They were both very young—not more than about twenty-two by Earth reckoning.

"Hi," said the girl.

The boy carried an instrument that looked like a mandolin. "We are the Friends of the Ways, Idris Hamilton. Welcome to our party."

Before Idris could say anything, the taped voice announced: "You are now approaching Vorshinski City."

The car stopped at Vorshinski. Three more young people boarded it, one of them a girl. They were obviously well acquainted with the two who had leaped aboard at Vorshinski Power. Besides the new intake of the Friends of the Ways, four middle-aged people—shift-workers probably—boarded the car. They viewed the young people with evident distaste and sat as far away from them as possible.

All four of them got off at Brandt Hydroponics.

The girl who had boarded at Vorshinski City came to Idris and kissed him on the cheek. "Hello, Earth man. Would you break somebody's arm if you desired to possess me?" She laughed.

Idris was nonplussed. He did not know what to make of these youngsters.

A young man offered him a flask. "Drink," he said. "You have found the Friends. The Friends have found you. Drink."

"What is it?"

"The water of life. The drink of the Friends."

In fact, it was kafra, the Minervan substitute for brandy. Idris took a swallow from the flask and handed it back. The young man also drank, then passed it to the others.

The car slowed down at Brandt Farm. Two more Friends jumped skilfully aboard.

"The androids who stepped out at Brandt Hydro will by now have reported that you are with the Friends," said the young man who had offered the kafra. "One of them was my mother."

"Why do you call them androids? They seemed quite

144

ordinary people to me."

"Because they accept and do what they are told to accept and do. They have lost a little of their humanity."

"Will it matter that they have reported what I am doing?"

The young man shrugged. "Not to us. Possibly to you . . . You, Idris Hamilton are regarded as a threat to society. We are tolerated as fools. Drink." Again he offered a flask of kafra. "My name is Egon. You are my brother."

"Thank you, brother," said Idris with sarcasm. "Will you be my brother when they want to lock me up again?"

"Your brother now and for always," said Egon. "You are our captain. You will tell us what to do."

At Aragon City more Friends boarded the car. They brought more kafra, more musical instruments.

The boy who had the mandolin started strumming and began to sing a ballad.

"The last man of Earth, yea, yea.
What is he worth? Yea, yea.
Will he lead us back to life,
Even if it brings us bloody strife?
Yea, yea, yea!

The last man of Earth, yea, yea,
Idris Hamilton got rebirth, yea, yea.
He got rebirth to set us free,
to give the Green Planet back to you and me.
Yea, yea, yea!

The last man of Earth, yea, yea.
We know what he's worth, yea, yea.
He's worth the living and he's worth the dying.
We'll follow him and there'll be no crying.
Yea, yea, yea!"

At Chiang City Damaris de Gaulle stepped on to the car. "Captain Hamilton," she said, "I love you. You are truly the Jesus Freak."

28

IT WAS A long night. The monorail car went round the circuit of the Five Cities—Talbot, Vorshinski, Brandt, Aragon, Chiang—several times before Idris had finally had enough and felt it was time to return to Mary.

Before the party broke up, he had drunk much kafra and talked with many young people whose names and faces he could only vaguely remember. It was true that they saw him as a saviour, a Jesus Freak. They wanted him to pull a rabbit out of the hat, destroy the *status quo* and build an expanding society. But, despite the words of the ballad and the protestations of the Friends of the Ways, he knew that they did not seriously expect him to lead them back to Earth. Basically, they only wanted a greater freedom than the present rigid society of Minerva afforded.

But they were too weak to organise themselves effectively to do anything about it. Like children, they wanted someone they could trust to lead them. Like children, they wanted to be told what to do. But would they have the nerve to do what was necessary? Would they be resolute enough to use force—if necessary? Would they be prepared to seize key installations—the power plants, the hydroponics units, the farms—and hold the Councils of the Five Cities to ransom to achieve their aims? Idris looked at them, and doubted it very much.

With only a hundred Earth men, Idris knew that he

could have controlled the entire Five Cities complex. But not even with a thousand of the Friends of the Ways could he hope to force the Triple-T faction, the fossilised power structure, to allow Minervan society to enter an expansive phase. It looked as if *Talbot's Creed* had achieved one thing, at least. It looked as if aggression, the love of adventure, the compulsion to go always one step further, had been successfully erased from the mind of man.

These effete young people simply wanted their Jesus Freak to perform tailor-made miracles. They didn't want any mess, they didn't want any conflict. They just wanted a painless, bloodless revolution. A miracle.

As the night wore on, Idris noticed that two or three of the original Earth children he had taken aboard the *Dag* for Mars had joined the Friends of the Ways. At first he felt glad. Here was hope. But after he had talked to them, he became depressed. They too, had succumbed to the subtle Minervan programming. When he had suggested that it might be possible to capture and hold the key personnel of one city and use that advantage to intimidate the administrations of the remaining four, they recoiled, horrified. Violence was out. Not just killing, but any kind of violence. They, too, wanted the Jesus Freak to walk upon the face of the water.

Idris returned to Mary Evans, dispirited, tired, a little drunk. She was deeply asleep. Subtle odours of sex still lay about her. He woke her gently and made love. But this time it was a totally mechanical action, aimed only at providing some sense of release, aimed only at providing oblivion. He said little, but she sensed his mood and responded as best she could. She knew that her body was not strong and young, as Zylonia's must be; but it was enough for her to be held by a man of Earth and know that he held her close because she, too, was of Earth. It was a great consolation.

The following morning he had an early visitor, an oldish man who seemed to have an uncanny resemblance to Manfrius de Skun, and who introduced himself as Harlen Zebrov.

147

He asked to talk to Idris privately.

"Can you not say what you have to say in front of my wife?" he demanded brusquely.

It was the first time he had referred to Mary as his wife. He had done it deliberately. It caused Harlen Zebrov to wince, and also caused Mary's eyes to glisten.

"Here on Minerva, we have time-pairing, as you must know, Captain Hamilton. The term wife has no meaning for us. And, incidentally, Mary Evans is not even your registered time-partner. However, that is not important. To answer your question: our discussion may certainly take place in the presence of Mary Evans. But I do assure you there are certain things it is safer and wiser for her not to know. However, the decision is yours."

Despite the resemblance to Manfrius de Skun, Idris had taken an immediate dislike to his visitor.

"As *you* must know, Mr. Zebrov, I am an Earth man and a qualified space captain. As such, I am empowered to marry any two consenting Earth people whether I am in command of a vessel or not." He turned to Mary. "Do you, Mary Evans, of your own free will, in the presence of this witness, take me, Idris Hamilton to be your lawfully wedded husband?"

"I do," said Mary. Somehow, as she spoke, her breasts were no longer soft. They became proud and high. Idris marvelled at the residual magic that still persisted in those few ancient words.

"I, Idris Hamilton, of my own free will, in the presence of this witness, take you, Mary Evans, to be my lawfully wedded wife. And I, Idris Hamilton, qualified space captain, nationality Australian, by mandate of the United Nations Organisation of Earth, now declare us to be man and wife." He grinned. "I have no ring, Mary. But a ring is not necessary according to Earth law. Customarily, at this point, the bridegroom kisses the bride. I will avail myself of this privilege."

"I love you," said Mary.

"Sweet, you have just married a terrible man. But I will

try to do my best for you. Believe that." He kissed her.

"I believe it."

"Charming," said Harlen Zebrov. "But this quaint ceremony has no relevance on Minerva."

"Do you believe in justice, Mr. Zebrov? Do you believe in upholding the law?"

"I do. That is why I am here to talk to you."

"Then you must realise that, according to interplanetary law, specifically the Agreement between U.N.O. Earth, the Lunar Commission and Mars Council of AD 2019, Mary Evans has now become my wife. I have been—shall we say—absent for five thousand years. But I do not think this Agreement was ever rescinded. My wife will remain present during our discussion. In fairness to you, I will remind you that under interplanetary law, she cannot, under any circumstances, be required to testify against her husband."

Harlen Zebrov laughed. "Captain Hamilton, you live in a dream world."

"No, sir. I live on Minerva. And I claim the privileges of a citizen of Earth under interplanetary law."

"But all that is ancient history to us."

"Must time corrupt justice, Mr. Zebrov? Now say what you have to say in the presence of my wife."

"First, I wish you to understand that what I have to say is not intended to be offensive. It is intended only as a statement of the Minervan point of view—and as a warning. Do I make myself clear?"

"You do."

"Good, then. Although I hold no political office, I am a prominent member of that group of Minervans who wish to preserve all that is good in our society. We are called, as you doubtless know, the Triple-T party. You have read the *Creed*, I understand, and therefore you must know our basic philosophy. Garfield Talbot was a great man; and his ideas and standards have stood the test of time.

"The point is, Captain Hamilton, that we have developed a stable, harmonius and virtually non-violent society. But that harmony is beginning to be threatened. It is threatened by your very existence. You are the product of a violent and self-destructive culture; and, regrettably, you have already demonstrated that you retain your capacity for violence. This disturbs and saddens most Minervans, but there are some for whom it has an unhealthy fascination. That is where the danger lies. We fear that—inadvertently, perhaps —your attitudes and beliefs might contaminate some of our younger and more impressionable citizens. Do I make myself clear?"

"I think so. You mean that you know I have met the Friends of the Ways. You smell a conspiracy."

Harlen Zebrov shrugged. "You are very blunt. I would not have put it like that. But I see we understand each other . . . Consider this, then. For thousands of years, your body was nothing but a desiccated piece of space flotsam drifting through the void in the wreckage of your last command. We Minervans restored you to life. Perhaps you will agree that you owe us something."

"Manfrius de Skun restored me to life. I agree that I owe him everything."

"Manfrius de Skun is dead, Captain Hamilton."

"Quite so. And you did not allow the techniques he developed to be used to restore him to life, did you?"

"We digress. That is a matter of Minervan policy—which you are neither competent to judge or to interfere with. I am assuming that you are sufficiently civilised to respect the values of our society. I am therefore asking you to give an undertaking not to renew your contact with the young and misguided people who call themselves the Friends of the Ways."

"It is illegal for me to talk to people I meet on monorail cars?"

Harlen Zebrov smiled. "You know it is not—at least, not yet. But I am sure we continue to understand each other. It is inadvisable. That is all."

"If that is all," said Idris calmly, "I will continue to exercise my freedom until it is curtailed. But thank you for your interest."

Zebrov sighed. "I felt it my duty to warn you . . . As you know, violent crime is minimal in the Five Cities, and we have no death penalty. But for serious transgressions, we do retain the power to exile. I think you should know that."

"Exile? Exile to where?"

"To the surface, Captain Hamilton. Where else? No one has been exiled from the Five Cities for a long time. It would be tragic if the next exile were to be you. Such a waste, don't you think? Such a waste of your second life and of the years Dr. de Skun laboured to restore sanity to a brain in a tank."

Idris felt murderous. He felt like taking Harlen Zebrov apart and spreading him in a thin film all over the floor. He mastered the desire with some difficulty.

"It was good of you to call on me, Mr. Zebrov," he said evenly. "I will think very carefully about what you have said."

"You will give the undertaking I require?"

"Allow me to think about it."

"Time is short, Captain Hamilton."

Idris smiled. "Time is always too short for all of us."

When he had gone, Mary said: "You know what he really means, Idris?"

"Yes, of course I do."

"I love you, and I don't want you to take risks. You have just declared me to be your wife. That makes me so happy. But please—please don't turn me into a widow."

He held her and kissed her. "Love, love, we must do what we can for Earth. I'll try not to make you a widow."

"I'm selfish," she sobbed. "I want you, only you."

"Then harden yourself, my dear. Because I am not willing to spend the rest of my days in this sepulchre they call Minerva."

29

FOR THE NEXT few days, Idris did nothing that could be construed as provocative. He spent his time exploring the Five Cities, sometimes with Mary and sometimes without her. He wandered from city to city by monorail, strolled apparently aimlessly among the central thoroughfares and gardens. He liked the city centres, though there was little variation. Each had its garden square, Council chambers, its hospital, its commissariat, its social centre. Each social centre was an amalgam of pub, disco, gymnasium, swimming pool, library and meeting room. Many people, he discovered, spent their entire free time at the social centres just as, in ancient times on Earth, many Romans spent their entire day at the baths. In each city the social centre was a forum for gossip, political argument, scientific and technological interchange, sexual and social reshuffling.

In many ways, Idris despised the Minervans. But in one way, they commanded his profound respect. They had exceptionally good manners—the like of which he had never seen on Earth or on Mars. They all knew who he was. His picture, his history, his recent actions had been on their screens and had obviously monopolised much of their discussion. Yet they respected his privacy. He was not mobbed, taunted, accosted. Generally, he was allowed to move about freely without feeling that all eyes were upon him. He was grateful. The only untoward encounter was when an elderly man, obviously drunk, offered to remove his old brain from his new body and drop it in the trash can where it belonged.

Idris accepted the old man's insults and refused to be provoked. Probably, he reflected, many Minervans would like to remove his brain and drop it in the trash can. From their point of view, he was an ungrateful wretch. He had been restored to life by immense effort and, so far, in their eyes, had only created trouble.

Before the old man could get violent, friends led him away. One of them, a woman, apologised profusely to Idris.

"Forgive him, Captain Hamilton. He has not only drunk too much, he is also overwrought. I am his current time-partner. If you wish to lodge a complaint, his name is Willem de Skun. He is the half-brother of Manfrius de Skun."

"Madam, I do not wish to lodge any complaint. I understand his mood. When he is more himself, please tell him that I am sorry if I offended him. His brother was a great man. I am bitterly sorry if in any way I was responsible for his death."

"You were responsible for the death of Manfrius," she said calmly. "By your actions, you ruined his life's work." She sighed. "But how could you, an Earth man, begin to understand the subtle politics of our society? I will tell Willem that you are sorry. He believed—as we all believed —that you care only for yourself."

"I care for myself, certainly," said Idris. "But I care more for mankind. Tell Willem that. Tell him also that Dr. de Skun was my friend, that he understood my attitudes even if he did not agree with them. Tell him that I, too, mourn the loss of a great man."

The exploration of the Five Cities and their communications system was not entirely haphazard, though Idris contrived to make it look so. He knew that he was being followed, that his actions and movements were being reported —probably to Harlen Zebrov. The Triple-T party was waiting for him to make a serious mistake.

Sometimes, he could detect the person who was following him. Sometimes, he was aware when the switch was made, and a new shadow took up the task. But, even when he could not identify his follower, he was aware all the time that someone was watching him closely.

He made his movements random so that the followers would not know his true intentions. He was making a mental map of the Five Cities. He would dearly have loved to commit the map to paper. But that would have been too dangerous. So the streets and avenues leading to monorail stations had to be memorised, and the map had to be an abstraction in his mind.

It was when Mary was with him that he made the most important discovery of all. The Five Cities formed a rough pentagon, and the monorail track linking them was roughly circular. But at Talbot there was a branch line. He had not noticed it before. Or, if he had, he had dismissed it as a branch tunnel to a repair shop.

While they were waiting at Talbot for a car, Mary said wistfully: "Wouldn't it be splendid to take a one-way trip down there, and find the *Amazonia* crewed and waiting for your orders?"

"Where does it lead?"

She was surprised. "To Talbot Field. I thought you knew."

He smiled. "Perhaps that was something they preferred me not to know. How far is it from here?"

"Seven or eight kilometres, I suppose. I don't know really. I have never been there . . . I must have made the journey once from the space-port to here, but I wasn't conscious at the time."

"Interesting," said Idris. "Love, we are being watched, so don't stare at that damned tunnel."

Zylonia de Herrens and Sirius Bourne boarded the same car.

"Hello," said Idris to Zylonia. "I'm breaking the rules, I know. But it won't be for long. I was sad to learn about the death of your father."

154

"You killed him," said Zylonia coldly. "You destroyed him and his work for nothing."

"I don't think I killed him. I understand he died of heart failure."

"You killed him. Violence spreads out from you like ripples from a stone thrown into water."

"I am sorry you believe that." He turned to Sirius Bourne. "I hope you will forgive my behaviour at Vorshinski Farm. I found it difficult to accept that you had a relationship with Zylonia before I did. I apologise for being so stupid."

"All that is past," said Sirius uncomfortably. "Let us live for the future, Captain Hamilton. I bear you no malice."

"May I introduce my wife," Idris said coolly. "Mary Evans, whom you must know, is now Mary Hamilton by ancient interplanetary law. This is no time-pairing. It is a one-to-one relationship that I will defend to the death."

Zylonia burst out crying. She and Sirius Bourne got off at the next station. Perhaps they had wanted to go there. Perhaps not.

30

In the end, in desperation Idris contacted the Friends of the Ways once more. He had worked out a plan—a crazy, half-cock notion of a plan—that would help his aims and theirs, if it succeeded.

If it succeeded. There was the catch.

If it failed, that would be the end of Idris Hamilton, the last Earth man. But there was one thing he was sure of: he could not resign himself to spend the rest of his days trapped under the rock of a frozen planet; trapped in a totally stable, totally frustrating society.

Better to accept the risk of exile—what but a sick society could claim to have abolished capital punishment but retained the right to exile a man to the surface where he must surely die?—than to face years and years of deadening inactivity, just existing for the sake of existing.

But he had no right to involve Mary in his enterprise—if, indeed, it ever came to anything—any more than she was involved already. If his plan failed and he was killed, Mary might still be allowed to live, provided she had played no part in the attempted coup. Whatever else they were, the Minervans were not deliberately vindictive. However, they would compulsively abort her baby because it was not 'authorised' and, doubtless, because they would be afraid of its genetic heritage.

So he told her nothing of his plan. Even Idris was

realistic enough to know that the odds against it succeeding were at least a hundred to one. He simply told her that he wished to talk again with the young people who called themselves the Friends of the Ways. He begged her to get a good night's sleep, for the sake of the child she carried, and promised to tell her all about his encounter next morning. Mary Hamilton, neé Evans, knew that Idris was engaged in something more than a social venture. But, in the short time that she had known him, she had come to trust him as well as to love him. He had made a woman of her. She knew that now, because she knew that she had not been fully a woman before. Also, he had given her hope. The least she could do in return was to give him unlimited trust. He was the last man of Earth, perhaps the last hope of mankind; and he had released his seed into her belly. It made her proud . . .

When Idris slipped out of the apartment, he was surprised to find the avenue totally deserted. Although it was in the middle of dim-out he had expected that a watch would be kept on his apartment; and it would have been difficult for an observer to hide in what was really no more than a long corridor whose starkness was relieved only by an occasional small tree with brilliantly variegated leaves.

He boarded a monorail car at Talbot. No-one was in it. Nor did anyone jump on at Talbot Farm, Talbot Hydroponics, or Vorshinski Power. He got off at Vorshinski City and waited for the next car. The station was deserted. Perhaps this was not one of the nights when the Friends of the Ways were meeting.

The next car contained two young men who might or might not be Friends of the Ways. Idris got on board, smiled vaguely at them and waited. They did nothing. At Brandt, Damaris de Gaulle and two more young men got on board. She spoke to them and to the two who were already in the car, then she came to sit by Idris.

"Hi, Jesus Freak. Last time round, you did not seem over impressed by our company. We were beginning to think maybe we had lost you. Were you disappointed by us?"

157

"Yes."

"Understandable." She laughed. "A homicidal Earth man is not likely to be impressed by a group of young people who seem to spend their time singing folk songs, drinking, making jokes."

"I am not a homicidal Earth man."

"Have you ever killed anybody?"

"Yes, but that does not make me homicidal."

Again she laughed. "Delicious Jesus Freak! It does, you know. How many people have you killed?"

"Three."

"Why?"

"They were saboteurs. They were trying to wreck a spaceship at Kennedy on Earth . . . It was a long time ago."

"You bet it was long time ago. But not subjectively for you. You are our homicidal Jesus Freak. Could we ask for more?"

At Brandt Hydro, three more young people boarded the car. They were obviously Friends of the Ways. One of them carried the inevitable mandolin, the others had flasks of kafra. Idris was able to put a name to a face—Egon. As before, Egon offered him the kafra.

"Drink, brother. It is good to see you again."

"Thanks, brother." Idris drank deeply. "Do you people play these childish night games endlessly, brother, or are there any among you willing to translate juvenile protest into harsh reality? I do not have much time, brother. I want to know if there are any among you who presume to be men?"

It was Damaris who answered him. "We play these childish night games, as you call them, so that our elders will think we are harmless. Only tell us what to do, Idris Hamilton, homicidal Jesus Freak of Earth. Only tell us what to do to destroy the stagnation that threatens us, and you will find the men you need—and the women, too."

The car stopped at Aragon. More people got on. Obviously young, obviously Friends of the Ways. Idris paid no attention to them. The boy with the mandolin had started to improvise another ballad about the last man of Earth. It was nauseatingly banal. Also somewhat out of tune.

"I have a plan," said Idris. "It requires about six resolute men—or women—who are willing to risk their lives in order to change for ever the destructive effect of *Talbot's Creed*. If you want an expanding society, it can be achieved. But some of you are going to have to take risks."

"What kind of risks?"

"You are going to have to risk your lives. What else? Get it into your heads that I am not going to perform any single-handed miracle, if that is what you were hoping for. I think I can help you and help myself. But I need backing. I need a few men or women who are not going to run home and put their heads under a pillow if or when the shooting starts."

"The Jesus Freak speaks big," said Damaris coolly. "Do any of us speak big also?"

"There will be shooting?" asked somebody.

"Not, I hope, in the literal sense."

"There will be killing?"

"Possibly. But I will avoid it if I can."

The monorail car stopped at Chiang City. Four more Friends of the Ways boarded it.

The boy with the mandolin started strumming:

"The last Man of Earth, he's here,
He's asking you to cast out fear."

"Abort," said Idris savagely. "There will be time for the song and dance routines later. Well, which of you totally secure brats will now look me in the eye and say he's prepared to risk his life for something he believes in?"

"Tell us your plan, brother," said Egon.

"Brother," retorted Idris, "I am not a fool. I will tell my plan only to those who sign ship's articles and are prepared to go for broke."

"What does that mean?"

"It means, my young friend, that I will not make my plan public. I will trust only those who trust me. They must back me with their lives, as I will back them with mine."

"At least," said Damaris, "tell us what you think you can

achieve. At the moment, dear Jesus Freak, it seems that you are asking us to follow you blindly."

"Fair comment. I will say this much, then. With the absolute backing of, say, six men and women, I think I can get us into a position where we can dictate terms to the Five Cities Council."

"What if they reject the terms?"

"They will not be able to afford to reject the terms," said Idris, "because the alternative will be the rapid destruction of Talbot City and quite possibly the other four."

"Man!" someone breathed. "This Jesus Freak thinks big. I mean big."

The boy with the mandolin stood up. He put down the mandolin, at the same time drawing something from the bulge of its base. The weapon he held looked very much like an ancient automatic pistol. He pointed it at Idris. Another of the Friends stood by his side. He, too, produced a similar weapon.

"Idris Hamilton, I arrest you in the name of the Five Cities Council. We know that you are strong and that you have skills of attack that have not been known on Minerva for thousands of years. But I hold in my hand an anaesthetising gun. We use it to stun pigs on the farms before they are slaughtered. Do not compel me to use it on you."

His companion stepped back and pointed his own gun at the others. They fell back.

Damaris de Gaulle refused to be intimidated. She was white-faced, furious. "We have always known there were traitors among us," she stormed. "So many of our projects were destroyed before we could operate them. But you, Egon! And you, Leander! This is too much!" She turned to Idris. "I am sorry, dear Jesus Freak. Truly, I am sorry."

"It was to be expected, my dear. It was to be expected." Idris laughed. "Despite my new body, I must be getting old."

The car began to slow down as it approached Talbot City once more.

"We will get off here, Idris Hamilton," said Egon. "I

must take you to my father, who will know what to do."

"Would his name be Harlen Zebrov?" asked Idris.

Egon smiled. "You have a quick mind. Too quick. It is a pity."

The car stopped. Idris put a hand to his head and partly covered his eyes. He swayed a little. "I feel ill."

"Then you shall have the best medical attention."

Suddenly, the hand shot out—flat, hard, devastating. It hit Egon in the throat before he realised what had happened. The force of the blow knocked him clean out of the car. There was a sickening thud. For a moment, everyone was frozen.

Then Egon's companion swung and faced Idris. "Animal!" But as he fired the anaesthetising dart, Damaris grabbed his hand and pulled. The dart pierced her breast. The young man seemed dazed by what he had done. Idris knocked the gun out of his hand and hit him relatively gently. He collapsed, moaning and coughing.

Damaris swayed. "Dear Jesus Freak. You *are* homicidal. Violence comes to you like —" She fell unconscious.

Somebody shouted: "Stop the Ways! Stop the Ways!"

Someone leaped on to Talbot platform and hit the emergency button that would halt the following car.

Three of the Friends of the Ways were already climbing down into the shallow pit under the monorail to reach Egon. Idris joined them.

There was nothing anyone could do for Egon. His head, evidently, had hit the rail on the way down. His neck was broken, and his head was smashed. Not even the genius of a Manfrius de Skun could bring the son of Harlen Zebrov back from the dead . . .

"You killed him! You killed him!"

"Murderer!"

"Beast!"

"Earth animal!"

Idris felt deadly tired. It was not, he realised, a good time to feel deadly tired. "Earth animal, yes," he agreed wearily. "Murderer, no. You saw what happened. I intended to disarm him, not to kill him. According to Earth law, I am guilty of manslaughter, not murder."

"This time, it will be exile."

"We were wrong ever to think you would help us. You are a destroyer, Earth man. Your people destroyed their own planet. Now you would destroy ours."

Idris climbed out of the pit and faced them on the platform. "Well, then, I am a destroyer. So come and get me, children. There are enough of you. But it will be costly. That I can promise you. It will be costly."

A girl stepped forward. "So, you invite more violence, Idris Hamilton. Your appetite for death is not yet satisfied. I little thought I would ever have to admit the Triple-T are right."

"Stop making speeches and get Damaris to a doctor," he said. Out of the corner of his eye, he saw that one of the young men had started thinking again and had picked up the anaesthetic gun that was on the floor of the monorail car.

He leaped back into the monorail pit as the man pressed the trigger. The dart exploded against the wall of the tunnel.

Idris crouched under the car, which gave him temporary protection, thinking what to do next. His mind worked furiously. Only a few metres away was the branch tunnel that led to Talbot Field. Could he make it before the bright boy put him to sleep with the gun? Should he even try to make it? Because, if he did, they would know where he had gone and what he was trying to do.

Someone called: "There is no escape for you now, Earth animal. Even you must know there is no hiding place on Minerva. You are routed for exile."

If I make a run for it, thought Idris, and if I head up the main tunnel, and if the boy with the gun doesn't hit me, they will think I'm running towards Brandt. Then if I wait a little until they have left Talbot, and then double back, there is a sporting chance I can get up the branch tunnel. There were too many goddamned ifs. They were bound to leave someone on watch at Talbot.

The boy was right. There was no hiding place on Minerva.

But what else was there to do?

162

The time had come to stop thinking and to trust to instinct. He made the run towards the tunnel leading to Brandt. Two more anaesthetising darts hit the wall very close to him. But he made the tunnel and kept on running for, perhaps, a hundred metres.

If they have any guts, he thought, they will come in after me and finish it off now.

But they haven't any guts, he told himself reasonably. These are spoonfed kids who have never known violence. They haven't any guts. None of them would want to come into the tunnel, even with an anaesthetic gun, to face an Earth man who had nothing to lose. So they would organise a reception committee at Brandt and possibly leave a holding guard at Talbot.

He would have to take his chance with the holding guard.

But strangely, they left no holding guard at Talbot. Clearly, they were unused to hunting criminals. They evidently thought that a criminal would do exactly what he was supposed to do, or what he had shown he intended to do.

Cautiously, after a time, Idris crept back to Talbot. Egon's body had been removed. But no one had been left on watch.

He emerged from the tunnel, inspected the station carefully, then began to walk up the branch tunnel to Talbot Field. After a few minutes he began to run. It occurred to him that, after a time, even the Minervans would realise what he was trying to do.

He was right. And he had already run out of time. As, puffing and exhausted, he approached the platform that could only be Talbot Field he saw that they were waiting for him.

Another anaesthetic dart whanged against the tunnel wall. He doubled back. But the monorail cars were in service once more. One from Talbot Field began to follow him. He ran until he could run no more.

The anaesthetising dart was a blessed relief. At least it stopped the dreadful pain in his chest.

31

THE TRIAL WAS over. It had been a fair one by Minervan standards—if less than fair by Earth standards. On the Earth Idris had known, violence had been, alas, no rarity. Because of this it was possible for terrestrial judges to consider the facts of violence dispassionately and to make, where the facts seemed to indicate it, a fine distinction between murder and manslaughter. On Earth a verdict of murder would be given only when the prosecution had established beyond all reasonable doubt that the accused had intended to kill. But on Minerva, where crimes of violence were almost non-existent, the act of striking a person in order to render him or her helpless could readily be construed as an intention to kill.

Minervans abhorred violence. Two civilisations had been destroyed by it; and their reaction to it was almost hysterical. If Idris had not had a recent history of violence—minor by Earth standards—and if he had not been, unintentionally, the symbol of a political and sociological struggle, he might have escaped with a long sentence of imprisonment and psychiatric treatment. But, in Minervan eyes, he had manifested an appetite for violence almost from the time he had been fully in control of his new body. From that proposition it was but a short step to establishing that he was a programmed killer.

Idris was defended by Erwin von Keitel, a close friend

and scientific colleague of the late Manfrius de Skun. But Dr. von Keitel interpreted his role not so much as defending counsel for an Earth man accused of murder but as advocate of the lately abandoned immortality project. With a friend like von Keitel, Idris concluded ruefully, he did not need any enemies.

The prosecution, an able exponent of Triple-T philosophy, destroyed von Keitel's arguments with negligible effort. It did not matter too much. The tribunal, consisting of the Presidents of the Five Cities was, as Idris saw from the start, a hanging tribunal. They had reached their verdict before the trial began.

He was prepared for the death sentence that was, in Minervan terms, not quite a death sentence. It came as no surprise.

Before the sentence of exile to the surface was carried out, his treatment was not bad. By Earth standards, it was highly civilised, if not luxurious. His apartment was little different from a standard living-module; but it was heavily guarded. Two men with anaesthetic guns were permanently on duty outside the door, which, strangely, was not locked. However, they had orders to shoot instantly if the door was opened from the inside without Idris having first asked permission over an intercom. A third man was available if Idris wished to play chess, talk or make any request. He was the only man allowed to approach within two metres of the prisoner. He was unarmed. He was also the most skilful gymnast on Minerva and an authority on the ancient art of judo.

Idris was allowed visitors; but only if they requested to see him. The tribunal had granted him ten M-days before exile.

How do you make the best use of your last ten days of life? He did not know. He had already passed once through the trauma of dying. But, until the bomb went off on the navigation deck of the *Dag Hammarskjold*, he had given little thought to the enigma of death. And when death came it had been mercifully quick. So now he was just as baffled as any man who has to face the prospect of certain and imminent extinction.

Mary visited him daily. Damaris came to see him once. Zylonia came to see him once—having, apparently, circumnavigated the order against personal contact. In any case, it could not matter now. The Earth animal would not be a threat to the social stability of Minerva much longer.

Mary's first visit was harrowing; but after a brief, semi-hysterical outburst of anguish she managed to regain control of herself. Thereafter she managed to maintain if not a mask of cheerfulness at least an outward show of calm acceptance. Idris felt doubly sorry for her. After he had gone there remained for Mary the ordeal of abortion. He knew that, physically, it would not be much of an ordeal; but he was afraid for her of the spiritual pain. He knew that, despite the somewhat flippant ceremony he had performed, she truly regarded herself as being married to him. To have her husband executed and then to have the child she was carrying destroyed would be enough to break most women, he thought. And she was the last true Earth woman married to the last Earth man and carrying the last Earth child. Poor Mary. Death—or exile, as they chose to call it—would be relatively quick for Idris. Then Mary would be left with much to endure.

They talked about it.

"I think I shall probably kill myself," said Mary calmly. "I don't want to live without you. Until you married me, Idris, I wasn't very much alive anyway. Afterwards . . ." she faltered. "Afterwards it will be worse."

"Love, I would prefer it if you didn't kill yourself. There is still Earth blood here on Minerva . . . There is still hope."

"The children?"

"Yes, the children. But children no longer. There are, perhaps, one or two young men who might —"

"You would want me to do that?" she demanded fiercely.

"If you could . . . If you would . . . Can you understand, Mary?" He took her hands. "I don't want to go topside knowing that the last hope for Earth goes with me . . . You can carry another child—legitimate and Minervan, by

166

Minervan standards—but it would be a true Earth child, and you could ensure that it remained a true Earth child. So long as the blood continues, there is a chance."

She said nothing, because there seemed nothing to say. Instead she took off her clothes and told herself that it did not matter that there were men with anaesthetising guns outside. Compulsively, idiotically, as they made love, she tried to will his semen to penetrate every cell of her body. So that Idris Hamilton, man of Earth, would remain alive in her flesh.

The visit from Damaris de Gaulle was brief.

She brought him a bunch of flowers—strange, fragrant Minervan flowers that looked like some kind of combination of terrestrial rose and carnation, which, quite possibly, they were.

"To get these, I had to promise to time-pair with a man at Brandt Hydro," she said lightly. "They are quite long-lasting. I hope you like them."

"I like them very much." The fragrance was sweet, but not overpowering.

"They were bred from Martian flowers. But, of course, all the flowers of Mars came from the gardens of Earth . . . Will you do something for me, dear Jesus Freak? Will you take one bloom with you when you are exiled."

"If it will please you."

"It will please me very much. There is a legend, you see. According to the legend, when one of these flowers dies another instantly blooms." She gave a nervous laugh. "Now you will regard me as just a stupid Minervan girl who wants to salve her conscience with an empty myth."

Idris smiled. "Wrong again . . . I never was your Jesus Freak, Damaris." He kissed her on the forehead. "But the flower legend is a good one. I like it."

Her attempt at calmness disintegrated. "If it were not for me," she sobbed, "you would not now be under sentence of exile. Forgive me, Idris Hamilton. Forgive me for asking you to meet the Friends of the Ways. Forgive us all for being ineffectual children. We want to change things, but we are afraid of paying the price. We have caused your destruction."

"Nonsense," he said. "I was already routed for destruction. You must know that. Because I am what I am, I was already on a collision course with Minervan values . . . It would have happened anyway, sooner or later. What I regret most of all is that Manfrius de Skun gave the best part of his life to bringing me back from the dead. He was ill rewarded . . . Yes, I like your flower legend. I believe it. I may die but, somehow, Earth will live."

"Goodbye," said Damaris. "I must go now. I am sorry. I am a coward."

"Goodbye, Damaris." He glanced at the flowers. "I will take the red one. It reminds me of an English rose. And when it dies, I will believe that another will instantly bloom."

The encounter with Zylonia was no less harrowing.

"Greetings, Idris."

"Greetings to you, Zylonia. How is Sirius? I hope he bears me no ill will."

"He is unhappy for you. He asks your forgiveness."

Idris raised an eyebrow. "But there is nothing to forgive. It was I who injured him."

"He asks your forgiveness," said Zylonia, "because he did not fully understand . . ." she faltered. "Because he did not fully understand how an Earth man would feel about a woman he had possessed—in Earth fashion."

Idris gave a deep sigh. "You remember when I asked you to take off your clothes? It seems a long time ago."

"I remember. And it is not very long ago."

Idris shrugged. "It is—in subjective terms. I fell in love with you then."

"Do you still love me?"

"Yes. But not as I did. Dreams die, Zylonia. New dreams are born. Now I regard myself as married—in the Earth sense—to Mary Evans. She is a good woman, and she is an Earth woman. Between me and her there exists something that could never have existed between me and you. Do you understand?"

"I understand."

"Well, then. Look me in the eyes, Zylonia, whom I loved and still love. Look me in the eyes and swear that you will do everything possible to stop Mary having her baby—the last Earth child—aborted."

Zylonia could not look him in the eyes. She covered her face with her hands. "I will do all that I can, Idris. I can promise nothing. But I will do all that I can."

"That is enough," he said tranquilly. "I no longer expect miracles. But I hold you to your word . . . I am sorry about your father. Plainly, he wasted himself upon me. For that I am truly sorry . . . Tell Sirius Bourne that my ghost will haunt him if he does not make you happy."

"Farewell, Idris."

"Farewell, my love. And thank you."

The last visitor of all was Mary. She gave herself to Idris, freely, desperately, joyously. She tried to distract him from watching the clock.

She succeeded.

When the man with the anaesthetising gun opened the door and pointed his weapon, Idris barely had time to realise that time—his time—had come to an end.

32

IDRIS AWOKE TO find himself lying on a trolley, such as might be used in a hospital. He was in a plain, unfurnished room whose walls were of metal. There was a module with a V-screen, a clock, a communicator, a pressure meter and a control panel, fixed on one wall. There was also a space suit hanging from a hook with two life-support packs lying close by it. A single red flower lay on one of the packs.

Idris sat up and waited for his head to clear. He already knew the kind of room he was in. He had used them many times before. He was in an air-lock.

He pulled himself together and stood up. As he did so, the V-screen came alive, and the face of Harlen Zebrov appeared.

So he had been under observation and they had been waiting for him to regain consciousness.

"Captain Hamilton," said Zebrov, "it is my duty to inform you that, in accordance with the orders of the Grand Council of Minerva, the sentence of exile is now being carried out. You are in the air-lock of Talbot Tower. In one hour from now—or less time upon your request—the air will be evacuated from this chamber and the door leading to the surface of Minerva will be opened. You may, if you require, demand one extra hour for the purpose of preparation. If you require this extra time, you must make your demand known within the next half-hour. If you have any other lawful and reasonable requests, please make them known as soon as possible. If you are unfamiliar with the equipment with which you have been provided, a technician is available to answer any questions. Both life-support packs are good for ten hours. Do you read me?"

"I read you, loud and clear. I am sorry about your son, Zebrov."

"Thank you. The prerogative of mercy does not lie in my power, Captain Hamilton."

Idris became angry. "I am not asking for mercy. I got my sentence from a hanging tribunal. I know better than to ask for a playback."

"Please, I do not understand you."

"No matter. I am sorry about your son, that is all. I hope you will believe that."

"I will try to believe it, Captain Hamilton. Now, are there any requests you wish to make?"

Idris thought for a moment or two. Then he said: "Will you give my thanks to Damaris de Gaulle? Tell her that the flower and the legend are greatly appreciated."

"Request granted."

"Will you also tell my wife that I think of her with deep affection and that I am sorry I have caused her such unhappiness? Tell her, too, that I believe that Earth will endure and that once again mankind will flourish upon its fertile lands."

"You have no wife under Minervan law, Captain Hamilton. But, of course, I know the person to whom you refer. Request granted."

"And will you assure me that no harm will come to Mary because of me? She was not in any way responsible for my actions."

"No action will be taken against Mary Evans, though, as you will recall, she was legally responsible for your good behaviour. The Grand Council feels that your sentence of exile is in itself sufficient punishment. Have you any further requests?"

Idris managed the ghost of a smile. "I would like to

171

borrow your space-ship to exile myself to Earth."

"Permission denied," said Harlen Zebrov without a flicker of expression. "I will now break contact. Unless you open communication once more within the next forty-five minutes, the air-lock will be evacuated. Goodbye, Captain Hamilton."

"Goodbye, Zebrov. Who knows—one of these days you may wake up and realise what you and your Triple-T friends have done to mankind."

The screen darkened. Idris, with the method of years of discipline, began his inspection of the space-suit and the life-support packs. Technology had developed greatly in the five thousand years since his first death. The equipment was vastly superior to anything he had ever known.

Damn these Minervans! They had immense talent and refused to make proper use of it. They could have done so much but they preferred to sit in their underground cities like troglodytes. Though their science was immensely sophisticated, they had allowed themselves to regress to a primitive condition. They had become afraid of everything, including themselves.

For a short time, Idris was tempted not to put on the space suit. When the air-lock was evacuated and the door opened, death would come very quickly. Perhaps it was better to end that way than to wander about on the surface, counting the hours and then the minutes until the life-support systems failed. Would he have the guts to pull the plug before that happened, or would he want to go to the last gasp of fetid air? He did not know. How could a man ever really know?

But he realised that, in his last hours, he wanted to look at the stars once more. The stars, to an experienced space-man, were almost personal friends. Beacons of the night that gave him a sense of location. Far, lonely torches, reminding him that he was not alone, that other sentient races existed—with problems as great or greater than those which confronted him personally and his people as a whole.

Yes, the stars were personal friends. By their very distance and remoteness they would remind him that, despite the

172

interval of five thousand years and despite the fact that the Minervans were descendants of refugees from Mars, they were of the same blood as Idris Hamilton. Earth blood. For what is a mere five thousand years in star time?

So he checked both life-support packs, familiarised himself with the connection mechanisms, clipped one pack on the back of the suit, tested the seals, got into the suit and made ready to go out on to the surface of Minerva.

It would be interesting—very interesting—to take a walk on the surface of the tenth planet, he hold himself.

When he had got himself ready and checked once more that his equipment was in order, he sat on the trolley and waited patiently for the external door to open. The door that would open to eventual oblivion.

33

THE FIVE ATOMIC lamps, each on top of a pylon three hundred metres high close to a city tower, shone brilliantly like fixed miniature suns.

Idris smiled to himself and peered rapturously through his visor at the bleak glory of the surface of the tenth planet.

Hans Andersen, he thought. The Ice Queen's Palace. Complete with diamonds as big as the Ritz. Where did that phrase come from? Ah, yes. Scott Fitzgerald. A twentieth century American writer . . .

Only the diamonds were not crystalline carbon. They were crystalline forms of oxygen and nitrogen. They caught the light from the atomic lamps and flashed as if they, too, were generating fire. It was like Guy Fawkes night, the Fourth of July, Bastille Day. With every step he took the crystalline rocks glittered and flashed in icy splendour, for kilometre upon kilometre. It was as if the entire planet were laying on an immense fireworks display—the greatest ever seen—to mark the passing of the last Earth man.

The atomic lamps had been turned on the moment Idris had stepped out of Talbot air-lock. Perhaps the Minervans thought he would be more afraid to die in the dark. They were not spacemen. They could not know that darkness and a skyful of stars were home to a spaceman. They could not know that, apart from the sun and the terrestrial moon, the stars were the oldest friends of man . . . Anyway, it was a nice gesture. The troglodytes meant well.

Far to the planetary north, there was another glow in the sky. It shouldn't be there, he thought hazily. It shouldn't bloody be there. There ought to be nothing but stars and cars and damned noisy bars thataways. Ooops!

Experienced spaceman that he was, he realised that he was getting rapidly drunk. "Only one iddy-biddy reason for that!" he said thickly to himself. "Oxygen bloody narcosis!"

The oxygen feed control and the meter were on the left arm of his space suit. He peered at it and saw that his oxy-nitro mix was far too rich. It was almost in reverse ratio. Perhaps he had absent-mindedly set it at that himself. Or perhaps not. Perhaps the bloody Minervans were trying to be kind. He turned the oxygen down. Goddammit, a man doesn't want to get pissed when he's about to die. Or does he?

Answer: No. Thought was still important. It was no good sinking into a state of euphoria while there were still several hours of life left in the tank. Besides, he still carried the spare pack. It felt damned heavy; but he wasn't going to jettison it. At least not yet. Not until he got tired of gazing at stars and sitting on rocks in the Snow Queen's Palace.

He wondered if he were under observation from any of the tower domes. Probably. Even though it was impossible for him to get back through an air-lock, the Minervans would not trust him to die docilely as required. It had been made abundantly clear at the trial that though, by Minervan standards, he was regarded as sub-human, he was also regarded as a very dangerous and unpredictable animal.

They had driven the tiger out, but they would not rest easy until they knew it was dead.

Well, he would not give them the satisfaction of seeing him die. They would have to come out and search for the body if they wanted proof. In any case, even then he could frustrate them. He could always throw himself into a hydrogen lake when he was ready to pull the plug. The weight of the suit and support pack should be enough to take him to the bottom, where he would lie, perfectly preserved for all eternity—or until the sun blew its fuses and destroyed the entire solar system.

Now that the oxygen and nitrogen mixture was back to normal, he was able to think clearly once more. He was able to consider his options. He had about eighteen hours of air left, he supposed.

So what were the options?

One: he could pull the plug here and now—to the immense relief of any watching Minervans. Two: he could take himself away from the illuminated areas, amuse himself for a while by exploring the extraordinary conditions on the surface of a planet whose temperature was only about sixteen or seventeen degrees above absolute zero, then pop into the nearest hydro-lake and perhaps leave behind him the legend of an immortal Earth man. Three: he could do something constructive.

But what the hell could be constructive in a situation like this?

The answer came almost as soon as he had formulated the question. He could head for Talbot Field. There were ferry rockets at Talbot Field, and the *Amazonia*. He knew that the space-ship was rarely used, and the ferry rockets only very infrequently. Therefore, there would only be a small duty staff. But, naturally, they would be alert to the fact that an Earth man was wandering about. So the chances of being able to pull a rabbit out of the hat were like those of the proverbial snowball in hell.

But the third option was better than nothing. Better than strolling about in ever decreasing circles until . . .

Besides, it would be good to see a space-ship again.

He switched on his head lamp and started to march—away from the atomic lamps, away from the planetary north where the glow in the sky marked the location of Talbot Field. No point in telegraphing his intentions. He would get out of visual range of the tower domes before he headed for the space-port. It occurred to him that the Minervans might have planted a radio beacon in his suit. Or they might simply track his movements by the atomic micropile that powered his heating circuit and lighted his head lamp. No matter. At least, now, he had a purpose. He would give them a run for their money.

His progress was slow. The ground was very uneven and some of the rocks—possibly igneous in origin—were razor sharp. If he tripped and his vizor hit one of those, all his problems would be over.

It took him the best part of two hours to get clear of the illuminated area.

He floundered through shallow puddles of liquid hydrogen and was amazed that the vacuum cells in the fabric of his space suit and the heating circuits protected him so efficiently from the external cold. The kind of space suits that were standard equipment on the *Dag Hammarskjold* would not have withstood such treatment. His legs would have frozen solid the moment he tried to wade through liquid hydrogen.

It was a fine clear night. A fine clear eternal night. There were a few fleecy hydrogen clouds in the clear helium sky. But, for the time being, there did not seem to be any prospect of rain or snow. Idris dreaded both. There were heating elements in his vizor, but he did not know if they were able to cope with a blizzard of hydro-snow. To be blinded at this stage would be damned near lethal.

He laughed aloud at the thought. Lethal, indeed! He was already a dead man, living on a few borrowed hours.

He looked at the stars, and was glad that they were still his friends. He picked out Polaris and silently sent it greetings. The greetings of a doomed Earth man.

To the north, the light in the sky was brighter. Goddammit, he would have to get over a range of hills.

A small range; but not cushioned by soil or grass like the hills of Earth. These, he knew, would be nothing but sharp rock with ice-caps of hydrogen and hydro-glaciers and outcrops of oxygen and nitrogen. The crystalline gases would be just as hazardous as the rocks themselves. One heavy fall and his problems would be over.

Somehow, he got over the hills. He was lucky. He found a small, narrow pass and trudged up a glacier towards it. Then the snow came. But it did not stick to his vizor.

And when he had negotiated the pass, he saw Talbot Field below him, about two kilometres away, its atomic lamp shining as bright as that goddammed star over Bethlehem.

34

Now HE STOOD by the field itself, an immense apron of smooth, heat-blasted rock, gazing at the small ferry rockets and the sleek, towering shape of the *Amazonia* that pointed like a vast phallic symbol to the stars. There was a considerable dusting of hydrogen snow on the ground; but the atmosphere was clear again. Which was unfortunate. Under the light of the atomic lamp, he could be seen clearly. So could his tracks in the snow, where he had wandered round the ferry rockets, looking hopefully and in vain for an unsealed air-lock. He had even tried the *Amazonia*. Its service ramp was down; but the air-lock mechanism was evidently designed only to open when some kind of identification tab or key was inserted in a slot.

Well, he had not expected them to make him a present of their only space ship. It was something to have got this far and to have seen the vessel that, one day, would lift off for Earth. That was something he had to believe. He didn't believe in God, but he had to believe in something. The unquenchable spirit of man was as good an abstraction as any. Some day, maybe not for hundreds of M-years, but some day, some bright Minervan young men would get fed up with living like moles. They would take the *Amazonia* and blast off for Earth or even Mars. It was a consoling thought. The one thing the Triple-T party could not do would be to make their sterile culture utterly and absolutely

179

stable. One day, then . . .

He was tired. He was very tired. And time was running out. He was on his second life-support pack. The first had failed in the hills and in a short snow storm. Fortunately, the snow had not been so thick that he could not see the warning red light that flashed on his arm panel. Changing a life-support pack was easy if you had a friend to help you. You just closed the umbilicus valve, lived patiently on your suit air and waited while your friend unhooked the dead pack, put the new one on your back and placed the fat cord in your hand so that you could snap it into position, check the seal, open the umbilicus valve once more and breathe freely.

To do it yourself in darkness in a hydrogen snow storm was rather more exciting. He had almost passed out before he could get the cord to the umbilicus. He was too far gone even to check the seal. Fortunately, it was perfect.

Then he had had to scramble down another bloody hydro-glacier, over an assortment of oxygen and nitrogen rocks as well as some bloody great igneous rocks. And, before he made the field, he had fallen head first into a fairly deep hydrogen pool. Despite the vacuum cells in the space suit and the heat provided by the overworked micro-pile, he had felt the cold. By the Lord Harry, he had felt the cold! It was so bloody cold he knew he would die within a few seconds. But somehow, blind and totally immersed in liquid hydrogen, he found his feet and started walking. Or wading. He walked out of the pool, a steaming bloody miracle, numb in his arms and legs and with hydrogen vapour wreathing about him like ghostly fingers of death.

It only took a short time for his visor to clear; and then, once more, his head lamp showed him the way forward.

And now here he was at Talbot Field, the end of the road. Well, it had been an interesting journey, worth making. He had seen the ship that would one day go back to Earth. Amen.

He judged he had about four hours of air left in the tank. Why didn't those bastards in the control tower come out and slap him on the back? It had been one hell of a journey.

180

He doubted if it could have been made by a Minervan. Only an Earth man would have been so stupid . . .

Why the hell hadn't they noticed him? Why had they let him prowl about the ferry rockets and try to get into the *Amazonia?* He was plainly visible. Why didn't they just come out and put a hole in his space suit and let him die like a gent?

Idris was angry. Unreasonably angry. He realised he was being unreasonable and automatically checked the oxygen-nitrogen mix. Normal. So it wasn't oxygen narcosis again. It was just the frustration of a man doomed to die. Hell, the least they could do would be to give him some small assistance. But, then, he reminded himself, the sentence had not been death. It had only been exile. Ha, ha! The Minervans made a fine distinction.

He looked at the control tower, and felt even more angry. He wondered if he could do any damage to those complacent zombies who were now, doubtless, observing him with clinical detachment.

He looked at the control tower and saw a light flashing.

He looked at it incredulously.

The sequence of flashes was regular. He understood it instantly. And didn't believe it. But the sequence was repeated again, and again.

It was a signal that was more than five thousand years old and that had been used and understood by seamen, airmen and spacemen of every nationality.

S.O.S.

35

IDRIS BEGAN TO run towards the control tower—which was a damn silly thing to do, he realised, over hydrogen snow. He fell twice and almost cracked his vizor. But he managed to get to the air-lock without killing himself. It was open and waiting.

He stepped inside. The manual controls were easy to operate. He closed the door, waited for the signal that indicated a perfect seal, then set the controls to pump out the deadly cold helium that was the surface atmosphere of Minerva. When that was accomplished, he punched the button that would fill the chamber with the standard oxygen/nitrogen mix and waited impatiently while the needle of the pressure meter rose.

With frantic haste, he unclipped his helmet and tore off his space suit. Suppose it was all a trick, some kind of sick joke, a misunderstanding, an illusion. Maybe on the other side of the internal door, there was a reception committee of fanatical Triple-T men, determined to finish him off before he could get up to any serious mischief with the space-craft.

He didn't care greatly. The only thing he was sure of was that the S.O.S. signal had not been an illusion.

What he found when he opened the door was the last thing he would have expected to find.

Mary—with an anaesthetising gun in her hand.

As soon as she saw him, she dropped the gun and rushed

to him, holding him fiercely, sobbing.

"Oh, Idris, Idris! I was so afraid you wouldn't make it." Then, despite the tears, she managed to smile. "But I knew you would, really. I had to believe you would . . . Otherwise, I couldn't have done it."

Bit by bit, he got the story out of her. She told it as they ran up a spiral stair-case to the control room. He hoped to live long enough to marvel at the sheer audacity of it all. But, for the time being, he could only register the facts.

She had managed to steal the anaesthetic gun from the woman who had been assigned to stay with her and keep her confined in her apartment until the sentence of exile had been carried out. She had put the woman guard to sleep, left the apartment and locked the door behind her. Then she had gone to Talbot station in the hope that she could find a monorail car that would take her up the branch line to Talbot Field. None seemed to be running. She waited till the platform was clear, then jumped down into the track pit and made her way along the tunnel to Talbot Field on foot. An empty car came when she was half-way up the tunnel. She lay in the pit and let it pass above.

The car stayed for a time at the Field terminus. When she arrived, she climbed on board, waited until it had started the return journey, then managed to wreck its auto-control system, which meant that it could not complete its journey down the tunnel and, consequently, that it would block any other car.

Then she had gone back to Talbot Field, taken the lift up to the control tower and had then wrecked that simply by breaking open the manual control panel and hammering the circuits with the butt of the anaesthetising gun. She got one hell of an electric shock in the process, but it had only stunned her momentarily.

She had not known how many men would be on duty in the tower; and, by that time, she was past caring.

She burst into the room, saw three men, and fired anaesthetic darts into each of them. Then there was nothing else to do but wait. And that had been the worst ordeal of all.

She had almost given up hope, and was resigning herself to the probability of her own exile, when she saw a white space-suit indistinctly against the hydrogen snow.

"I knew you would try to get here, Idris. You wouldn't just walk about until you died. You are not that kind of man. You would try to take the space-ship. I knew it . . . Did I do the right thing. I didn't think it all out. It just sort of happened."

"My love," said Idris, "you are magnificent. We may not beat these bastards, but we will give them a hell of a run."

In the control room, he found the three men. One was slumped by a computer console. The other two lay sprawled on the floor.

He examined the room carefully. He found three items of interest. The first, hanging on the wall, was the panel holding the electronic keys that would open the air-locks of the *Amazonia* and the ferry rockets. The second was a button behind a glass panel. There was a bronze plaque above the stud, which bore the following words: "If the existence of the Five Cities of Minerva is ever threatened, from whatever cause, I, Garfield Talbot, enjoin any Minervan present at Talbot Field to press this stud." And the third item was a hot-line to the office of the President of Talbot City.

"Mary, is there any other way to get up to the control tower from the monorail tunnel, apart from the lift?"

"I don't think so. There is a service ladder in the lift shaft, but I couldn't find any stair-case."

Idris gave a great laugh and kissed her. "Then it is going to take them some time to get to us. If they have to track over the surface from Talbot City, it will take hours and hours."

"They have jet sleds," said Mary. "They work on a hover-craft principle and can get over very rough terrain."

"Never mind. We'll see them coming. We can seal the air-lock if we have to. Then they would probably need laser equipment to break in . . . Mary, there is just a chance—not

184

much of one, but still a chance—that you may yet see the green hills of Earth. Keep your fingers crossed."

He read the words on the bronze plaque once more and stroked his chin thoughtfully. "I wonder what Garfield Talbot was up to when he had this thing installed? Whatever else he was, he was a very practical character. A good commander, I'd say. And a good commander plans for the safety of his troops and tries to foresee all possible threats. This panic button must be pretty damned important for it to be kept operational for three thousand years."

"If it is operational," said Mary. "It could just be maintained for sentimental reasons."

"I wish I knew what it was designed to do." He broke the glass and gazed silently at the stud as if sheer concentration would reveal its secret.

"You are not going to press it?" said Mary apprehensively.

He held her shoulders. "My dear, consider our situation. Sooner or later the Minervans are going either to force their way into here or to force us to get out. What can we do? Well, we have the key to the *Amazonia* air lock. We can take possession of the vessel. But I am damned sure that even if it is fully fuelled and provisioned, you and I can't crew it to Earth orbit; and even if we could there wouldn't be a hope in hell of making a soft touch-down. But let's suppose, by some miracle, we did make a soft touch-down. What do we do—become the latter-day Adam and Eve? We can't hope to accomplish much by ourselves, sweet. Genetics, accident, the laws of chance and every damn thing you can think of are against us. We need people."

"The Triple-T people won't ever allow any Minervans to leave," said Mary positively, "even if anyone wanted to."

"They might—given the right stimulus . . . Do the Minervans have any kind of game roughly similar to poker, Mary?"

"I don't think so."

"Good. I imagined they didn't. Poker is a game of bluff. It requires low cunning, deceit, an iron nerve—and a bit of luck . . . I used to be quite good at poker. . . . I didn't always win. But if you don't ever gamble you don't ever win. I want to gamble on Talbot's panic button, Mary. He was a tough old bird, hard as nails, crazy like a fox. But he was a practical man. Clearly, he knew that sooner or later, Minerva would face some kind of crisis, some kind of threat. I want to know what he has or had arranged to be done about it. Are you with me?"

She smiled. "Of course I am with you, Earth man. That is all that really matters." She read the plaque once more. "If the existence of the Five Cities of Minerva is ever threatened, from whatever cause, I, Garfield Talbot, enjoin any Minervan present at Talbot Field to press this stud." She was no wiser.

"I bet there are similar panic buttons in the Council chambers of the Five Cities," said Idris. "Talbot wouldn't have relied on having just one."

"Not that it really matters," sighed Mary. "There is no threat to the existence of the Five Cities."

Idris gave a grim laugh. "Oh, yes, there is. Me—plus poker."

He pressed the button.

36

THE ACCENT WAS strange but the voice of Garfield Talbot sounded loud and clear, though it must have been recorded thirty centuries ago.

"Citizens of Minerva, greetings. Wherever you are, whatever you are doing, my voice comes to you over a secondary communications network that was established for this very purpose. When we came to Minerva from Mars, we came as refugees from the social violence that destroyed two great civilisations. Our ideal was to create a stable society where violence of any kind would be abhorred. In my lifetime, I have seen that we are well on the way to realising that ideal; and I am content.

"As I speak these words, I cannot possibly foresee if you will be listening to them a few years from now, a few decades from now, a few hundred years from now, or, perhaps even longer. But I do know that you should not be hearing them at all unless the very existence of the Five Cities is threatened. It may be that you are facing some natural disaster or that social conflict is attacking the very stability we sought to achieve. It may even be, for reasons I cannot possibly anticipate, that you or some of you will find it necessary to leave this planet, perhaps seeking another refuge in the solar system.

"Therefore, know that the *Amazonia* is not the last spaceship on Minerva. It was said, and I have found it prudent never to deny it, that, with the exception of the *Amazonia*, the fleet that brought us here was destroyed by my orders. I have encouraged that belief so that my generation and its descendants would strive to make a success of life on this world rather than dream of journeying to another.

"But four of the original space vessels were not destroyed. They are the *Hellas,* the *Elysium,* the *Arcadia* and the *Utopia*. All are, of course, nuclear powered, deriving their fuel from the liquid hydrogen that is so abundant upon this planet. The vessels are stationed at the south polar region. Make such use of them as you need. If the time has come for some or all of you to leave this planet, go with the knowledge that Garfield Talbot realised that humanity would not be confined to Minerva for ever.

"But I say to you, whatever the threat that now faces Minerva, it is your duty to ensure that the race of man shall not perish and that it shall flourish to ultimately reclaim the glories that were lost. Now I, Garfield Talbot, bid you farewell."

Idris gazed at Mary. There was a glint of triumph in his eyes. "I told you I was a pretty good poker player. That was the ace I needed—Garfield Talbot!"

He grabbed the V-phone, the hot-line to the office of the President of Talbot City. The screen lit up. He saw the President's face.

"This is Captain Idris Hamilton. You have heard the voice of Garfield Talbot?"

"We have." The President looked tired, frightened, strangely shrunken. "What are you trying to do?"

"In the name of the people of Earth," said Idris, "I have assumed command of Talbot Field and of the *Amazonia*. Can you hook this line to the V-phones, screens and public address systems of the Five Cities?"

"We can—but why should we, Captain Hamilton? In a short time, your escapade will be terminated."

"Unless you do so, sir, in a short time Talbot City and quite probably the other four cities will be destroyed. You have five minutes."

"Captain Hamilton, you can accomplish this?"

188

"I can and will. You have four and a half minutes."

"Very well. We will take you at your word. We can hardly afford to do otherwise."

Idris glanced at the standard V-phone and the tri-di. "Get those things working, Mary. I don't think he will cheat, but let's be sure." He stood squarely in front of the hot-line lens so that his image would be clear.

"The connections are being made," said the President of Talbot City.

"You now have three and three quarter minutes," snapped Idris.

He waited.

Presently, the V-phone and tri-di both relayed his image.

"The link is complete," said the President.

"Thank you." Idris cleared his throat. "Citizens of Minerva, you have heard the voice of Garfield Talbot, whom you revere. Now hear what Idris Hamilton, man of Earth, has to say. I have command of the control tower at Talbot Field. In the name of the people of Earth, I have also assumed command of the *Amazonia* which I shall shortly board. There are two of us—myself and my wife, Mary. We cannot crew the *Amazonia* to take it to Earth, though we would dearly love to do so.

"However, we can and will lift off and set the ship down on top of Talbot City, and let the atomic engine go critical if we are attacked or if our demands are not met. Our demands are simple. We ask only for the freedom to seek a volunteer crew—a crew who, willingly, will help us to return to Earth and see if the planet is habitable once more. I believe it may be. Certainly, we should try to find out.

"You have lived so long below the surface of this planet that you are in danger of losing the sense of adventure, the greatness of spirit, the willingness to take risks that is the essence of the spirit of man. I am asking you to show that the greatness of mankind is not yet lost. In the name of the first ignorant savage to discover the use of fire, I am asking you. In the name of the primitive inventor of the wheel, I am asking you. In the name of that long-dead semi-human creature who found that a log would transport him across water, I am asking you. In the name of the first man who killed himself constructing a flying machine, I am asking you. And I am asking you in the names of the illustrious dead of Earth. Of Galileo, Copernicus and Kepler, who gave you knowledge of the stars. In the names of Leonardo, Rembrandt, Michelangelo, who fixed beauty and wonder upon canvas and in stone. In the names of Bach, Mozart, Beethoven, who brought the music of the spheres to men. In the names of Louis Pasteur, who helped conquer disease; Ernest Rutherford, who opened the door to atomic energy, Yuri Gagarin, who was the first man to venture into space.

"But these were Earth men, and you are Minervans, and your ancestors were Martians. So why should you be concerned with the fate of Earth? I will tell you why. Because the red blood of Earth still runs in your veins. Your ancestors lived on Mars for two thousand years. You have dug a rabbit warren here on Minerva and have survived for three thousand years. But you have only survived. You have done nothing else. And yet you carry the red blood of Earth. The blood of the first man who used fire, the blood of Leonardo, the blood of Gagarin.

"Garfield Talbot, who has his own claim to greatness, knew that there was a time to stay still and a time to go forth. Do not betray his heritage; but also do not betray the future of man.

"I will now take possession of the *Amazonia*. If none of you join us, we will not retaliate as threatened. We will lift from Minerva and route ourselves for Earth. I doubt that we shall arrive. But, as a poet whose name I fail to recall, once said: 'The journey is what matters.' Message ends."

Mary's eyes were wet with tears. "My love, I am so proud. You are the last Earth man, and I shall be proud to die in your company."

"You will not die," said Idris intensely. "You will not die. You are not allowed to die. There is something in your belly that has got to live. Now stop wasting bloody time and put on a space suit. We must lock ourselves into the *Amazonia* before those Triple-T characters recover their wits."

190

37

IDRIS SAT IN the command chair on the navigation deck of the *Amazonia*. He was waiting. Mary was securely hooked to the first officer's chair. It was going to be one hell of a lift-off, thought Idris. The *Amazonia* would probably turn turtle during the first ten seconds of ignition. And that would be the beginning and the end of the voyage to Earth.

Still, nothing attempted, nothing gained. It had been worth the effort. Some you win, some you lose. This one was lost. The Minervans had not responded, or the Triple-T had been too strong. Still, it had been worth the effort. And this was a better way to die than by running out of air on the surface.

He had kept the radio channels open. But so far there was nothing except static.

He glanced at the metres on the control console.

"Seven minutes to lift off," he said professionally.

Mary was silent for a while. Then she said urgently: "Idris, they are coming."

"Christ, woman, who is coming?"

"They are coming. Look."

He went to the observation panel, over which steel shutters would descend before ignition.

It was true. They were coming. He could see lights out on Talbot Field. Rapidly moving lights. Jet sleds.

But who was coming? A wrecking squad, most likely.

The radio gave him his answer. He heard the voice of Damaris de Gaulle.

"Hello, Jesus Freak. Hello, Jesus Freak. You have your volunteers. When one bloom dies, another is born. Do you read me?"

"I read you," said Idris. "I liked that legend very much. Assemble your volunteers, please, at the control tower. The lock is open."

He looked through the observation panel and saw the fairy lights—at least that is what they looked like—converging on the control tower.

He turned to Mary. "Destination, Earth?"

Perhaps, eventually, the other ships that Garfield Talbot in his wisdom had preserved would follow. Perhaps not.

But one, at least, would discover whether Earth, the third planet, would bloom again.

Suddenly, Idris had begun to believe in magic. When one flower dies, another is born.